THE CARNIVAL OF DEATH

SELECTED FICTION WORKS BY
L. RON HUBBARD

FANTASY
The Case of the Friendly Corpse
Death's Deputy
Fear
The Ghoul
The Indigestible Triton
Slaves of Sleep & The Masters of Sleep
Typewriter in the Sky
The Ultimate Adventure

SCIENCE FICTION
Battlefield Earth
The Conquest of Space
The End Is Not Yet
Final Blackout
The Kilkenny Cats
The Kingslayer
The Mission Earth Dekalogy*
Ole Doc Methuselah
To the Stars

ADVENTURE
The Hell Job series

WESTERN
Buckskin Brigades
Empty Saddles
Guns of Mark Jardine
Hot Lead Payoff

A full list of L. Ron Hubbard's
novellas and short stories is provided at the back.

*Dekalogy—a group of ten volumes

The
CARNIVAL
of DEATH

GALAXY
PRESS

Published by
Galaxy Press, LLC
7051 Hollywood Boulevard, Suite 200
Hollywood, CA 90028

Printed in the United States of America.

ISBN-10 1-59212-247-7
ISBN-13 978-1-59212-247-9

Library of Congress Control Number: 2007928017

10 9 8 7 6 5 4 3 2 1   2007

CONTENTS

Stories from Pulp Fiction's Golden Age

AND it *was* a golden age.

The 1930s and 1940s were a vibrant, seminal time for a gigantic audience of eager readers, probably the largest per capita audience of readers in American history. The magazine racks were chock-full of publications with ragged trims, garish cover art, cheap brown pulp paper, low cover prices—and the most excitement you could hold in your hands.

"Pulp" magazines, named for their rough-cut, pulpwood paper, were a vehicle for more amazing tales than Scheherazade could have told in a million and one nights. Set apart from higher-class "slick" magazines, printed on fancy glossy paper with quality artwork and superior production values, the pulps were for the "rest of us," adventure story after adventure story for people who liked to *read*. Pulp fiction authors were no-holds-barred entertainers—real storytellers. They were more interested in a thrilling plot twist, a horrific villain or a white-knuckle adventure than they were in lavish prose or convoluted metaphors.

The sheer volume of tales released during this wondrous golden age remains unmatched in any other period of literary history—hundreds of thousands of published stories in over nine hundred different magazines. Some titles lasted only an issue or two; many magazines succumbed to paper shortages during World War II, while others endured for decades yet. Pulp fiction remains as a treasure trove of stories you can read, stories you can love, stories you can remember. The stories were driven by plot and character, with grand heroes, terrible villains, beautiful damsels (often in distress), diabolical plots, amazing places, breathless romances. The readers wanted to be taken beyond the mundane, to live adventures far removed from their ordinary lives—and the pulps rarely failed to deliver.

In that regard, pulp fiction stands in the tradition of all memorable literature. For as history has shown, good stories are much more than fancy prose. William Shakespeare, Charles Dickens, Jules Verne, Alexandre Dumas—many of the greatest literary figures wrote their fiction for the readers, not simply literary colleagues and academic admirers. And writers for pulp magazines were no exception. These publications reached an audience that dwarfed the circulations of today's short story magazines. Issues of the pulps were scooped up and read by over thirty million avid readers each month.

Because pulp fiction writers were often paid no more than a cent a word, they had to become prolific or starve. They also had to write aggressively. As Richard Kyle, publisher and editor of *Argosy*, the first and most long-lived of the pulps, so pointedly explained: "The pulp magazine writers, the best of them, worked for markets that did not write for critics or attempt to satisfy timid advertisers. Not having to answer to anyone other than their readers, they wrote about human beings on the edges of the unknown, in those new lands the future would explore. They wrote for what we would become, not for what we had already been."

Some of the more lasting names that graced the pulps include H. P. Lovecraft, Edgar Rice Burroughs, Robert E. Howard, Max Brand, Louis L'Amour, Elmore Leonard, Dashiell Hammett, Raymond Chandler, Erle Stanley Gardner, John D. MacDonald, Ray Bradbury, Isaac Asimov, Robert Heinlein—and, of course, L. Ron Hubbard.

In a word, he was among the most prolific and popular writers of the era. He was also the most enduring—hence this series—and certainly among the most legendary. It all began only months after he first tried his hand at fiction, with L. Ron Hubbard tales appearing in *Thrilling Adventures, Argosy, Five-Novels Monthly, Detective Fiction Weekly, Top-Notch, Texas Ranger, War Birds, Western Stories,* even *Romantic Range.* He could write on any subject, in any genre, from jungle explorers to deep-sea divers, from G-men and gangsters, cowboys and flying aces to mountain climbers, hard-boiled detectives and spies. But he really began to shine when he turned his talent to science fiction and fantasy of which he authored nearly fifty novels or novelettes to forever change the shape of those genres.

Following in the tradition of such famed authors as Herman Melville, Mark Twain, Jack London and Ernest Hemingway, Ron Hubbard actually lived adventures that his own characters would have admired—as an ethnologist among primitive tribes, as prospector and engineer in hostile climes, as a captain of vessels on four oceans. He even wrote a series of articles for *Argosy,* called "Hell Job," in which he lived and told of the most dangerous professions a man could put his hand to.

Finally, and just for good measure, he was also an accomplished photographer, artist, filmmaker, musician and educator. But he was first and foremost a *writer,* and that's the L. Ron Hubbard we come to know through the pages of this volume.

This library of Stories from the Golden Age presents the best of L. Ron Hubbard's fiction from the heyday of storytelling, the Golden Age of the pulp magazines. In these eighty volumes, readers are treated to a full banquet of 153 stories, a kaleidoscope of tales representing every imaginable genre: science fiction, fantasy, western, mystery, thriller, horror, even romance—action of all kinds and in all places.

Because the pulps themselves were printed on such inexpensive paper with high acid content, issues were not meant to endure. As the years go by, the original issues of every pulp from *Argosy* through *Zeppelin Stories* continue crumbling into brittle, brown dust. This library preserves the L. Ron Hubbard tales from that era, presented with a distinctive look that brings back the nostalgic flavor of those times.

L. Ron Hubbard's Stories from the Golden Age has something for every taste, every reader. These tales will return you to a time when fiction was good clean entertainment and the most fun a kid could have on a rainy afternoon or the best thing an adult could enjoy after a long day at work.

Pick up a volume, and remember what reading is supposed to be all about. Remember curling up with a *great story.*

—Kevin J. Anderson

KEVIN J. ANDERSON *is the author of more than ninety critically acclaimed works of speculative fiction, including The Saga of Seven Suns, the continuation of the Dune Chronicles with Brian Herbert, and his* New York Times *bestselling novelization of L. Ron Hubbard's* Ai! Pedrito!

THE CARNIVAL OF DEATH

CHAPTER ONE

THE HEADLESS CORPSE

RISING to a crescendo of stark horror, a scream of death hacked through the gaiety of the night. It came from the sideshows, from directly beneath the lurid banner which depicted ferocious African headhunters at their feasting. In spite of the babble of the pleasure-seeking carnival crowd, the sound lingered eerily for an instant.

Gaming wheels stopped their monotonous whirring. Faces in the crowd grew blank and then frightened. The hardened barkers whirled in their stands and stared. The gay Ferris wheel stopped, its motor coughing and spitting in idleness. Grifter and rube alike—they all seemed to know that death stalked upon the midway.

Seven stands away from the lurid banner, Bob Clark, carnival detective, paused for a second, held by the seeping terror of the shriek. Into his steel-colored eyes came a look of certainty. Then, before the crowd had recovered from that first shock, Bob Clark began to run.

He rounded the corner of a tent and sprang up to a raised platform. The entrance gaped blackly before him. In the sudden hush he heard the sound of running feet and realized they came from within the tent. Whipping a flashlight from his pocket, he darted in.

The damp mustiness of the tent dropped upon him like a

3

cloud. He lunged into benches, tripped over ropes, sending the icy beam of his light to the uncurtained stage before him.

He skirted the edge of a pit, stumbled up a flight of steps, and stopped as suddenly as though he had come against a stone wall. His eyes dilated, and he felt a shudder course its cold way up his tingling spine.

Ringed by a pool of blood which seemed black in the white light lay a ghastly corpse. The hands were clutched in front of the torso; the legs were drawn up, twisted by unbearable agony. In spite of the years at his trade, Bob Clark shuddered again, for the body was without a head!

The flashlight whipped down into the pit to display its emptiness. Not long before, at the midshow of the evening, four African headhunters had been manacled there, savage creatures on display to all who had the necessary dime.

They had been ugly brutes, teeth filed to points, brown skins glistening under the glare of spots, faces inscrutable, eyes filled with evil. They had been brought straight from Africa for Shreve's Mammoth Carnival.

But now the irons gaped emptily, and the implication was plain. Entirely too plain. It was evident that the headhunters had escaped, and in escaping had murdered their barker, taking his head as grim payment for their captivity.

Clark jumped down into the canvas-rimmed hole. Bending quickly, he snatched up a steel wristlet and examined it, expecting to see the metal filed. He gave a low mutter of surprise when he found it was not. The wristlet was intact and had been opened with a key.

Back on the raised platform, Clark stepped gingerly to the

Ringed by a pool of blood which seemed black in the white light lay a ghastly corpse.

side of the headless corpse. He took a still-warm hand in his own and without effort parted the fingers and removed several strands of whitish hair they had clutched. He held these in the beam of his light, examining them. He frowned and thrust them into an old envelope.

People were coming through the entrance of the tent, cautiously and without a great deal of noise. Outside the carnival had begun its song again. Bob Clark looked at the entering barkers and property men and selected two, knowing that as carnival detective he had that right.

"Stay here with this, will you?" said Clark.

The first of the two selected was a flashily dressed ballyhoo man from an adjoining stand.

"Who?" he blurted tremulously. "You don't mean me. That guy's dead!"

"Sure he's dead," rasped Clark. "You'll stay."

The man started to protest and then saw the grim set of the carnival detective's jaw. With a glazed stare, the barker sat down on a folding seat. The property man designated stood with feet wide apart, disbelief in his eyes.

"But, good God, Clark," stammered the property man. "Those cannibals are loose! What if they come back?"

"They won't," said Clark with a grimace. "They're miles away from here by now."

"I wish I believed that," croaked the barker.

"So do I," snapped Clark, as he started toward the back of the tent.

To Bob Clark this murder assumed greater proportions

than a crime committed by four escaping headhunters. It was only a link in the chain he had tried so hard to break.

He had been with Shreve's Mammoth Carnival for three months, and during that time two distinct attempts had been made upon his own life. He had been at a loss to explain these because to his knowledge only one man with the show knew his true identity.

That man was beyond suspicion—he was Shreve, owner of the show. And Henry Shreve had been the one who had first informed the United States Government of the curse which rode with the outfit—the curse of dope.

That tip tallied with their own records, and the Treasury Department had not been slow in placing an operative on the case. That man was Robert W. Clark, of the Narcotics Squad, who, to date, did not have a single failure to his discredit.

Bob Clark knew that he walked on the brink of death, but he only shifted his light to his left hand and lifted the tent flap with his right. A blur of stakes and ropes was silhouetted against the murky sky as he looked up. He could see the fairgrounds' grandstand against the glowing clouds which hung over the large Middle Western town.

Then without warning a blackjack smashed down. It caught the detective a glancing blow on the side of the head and sent him reeling to one side, knocked the flashlight from his grasp. Dazedly, Clark flung out a hand, his clawing fingers clutched a sleeve. He pulled the arm savagely toward him, throwing his unseen assailant off balance.

In an instant the detective's head was clear. He raised the

flashlight in his left hand, brought it down viciously, and heard his foe grunt with pain as the lamp thudded against his shoulder.

They closed in. Tent ropes tripped him, death-seeking hands tore at him, the night spun crazily about him, but Bob Clark held on tenaciously. Blows pounded in his face, a writhing demon grunted animal-like in his grasp. A blackjack smashed again and again into his body.

Clark fought silently, his breath coming in great soundless gasps.

The detective's assailant wrenched his arm free, a fist smacked against Clark's chin. He felt himself hurtled backward with terrific speed. A rope was between his legs; he stumbled over it, crashed to the ground.

Before he could rise, his foe was on top of him, pounding him with crazed strength. Into Clark's mind darted a vision of headhunters, sharp knives and ripped bodies.

Doubling his knees, Clark managed to jam his feet against the other's chest. He thrust his legs out savagely, summoning every ounce of his strength. With a howl, his attacker catapulted back, hit the ground, rolled over and darted away.

Clark jumped up in pursuit, but his speed was his undoing. He crashed into a pile of stakes and went down, a sharp cry of pain tearing itself from his lips. Sprawling there, he found his dropped flashlight.

Battered and dented though it was, the light worked. Its beam flashed on, splashed off white canvas and red props and then caught a face in its glare.

The features were pinched and the eyes wide with fear. It

was a white man, young, with blond hair half hidden by a cap. Although the face was there but an instant, Clark's trained eye caught and held the image for later identification.

Before the detective could regain his feet and dash in pursuit, the face was gone. The dark blur of a body sped out of sight around a stand. Even though he knew the man would instantly be swallowed up in the surging crowd on the midway, Clark pounded in pursuit.

He slowed his pace to a walk when he reached the lighted area. To all outward appearances both grifters and customers had forgotten the tense atmosphere of horror created by the scream. Perhaps rumors had been circulated to stay possible panic.

Clark hoped so, because panic would go a long way toward ruining his chances of again coming to grips with his late assailant. The unknown man obviously had not been one of the headhunters.

The glimpse of that fear-distorted face had tightened the detective's hold on his one clue. He had seen the blond hair which might possibly match that which had been clutched in the hand of the headless corpse.

The detective felt something was behind the escape of the headhunters. Something which would somehow tie up with Clark's own task.

Someone had purposely released the headhunters. Clark was positive of that now, and he had to learn why. Someone had waited for him there by the tent. He had heard the footsteps when he had first entered. Someone knew why he was there.

But the show went on. Ticket takers might shake a little when they tore off their pasteboards; spielers might glance fearfully behind them into shadows where black death might lurk—but the show went on.

Once more all of the features of the midway were going through their routines.

Outside of one stand a pair of acrobats was doing a headstand while their barker gave his spiel of the more death-defying feats which would occur inside the tent.

A little further along a clarinet and bass drum throbbed the strains of "The Streets of Cairo" as an Oriental dancer went through her snakelike gyrations. With a steady hand, the knife-thrower stood beside his tremendous pile of sharp knives, selecting his blades carefully, and heaving them unerringly at his human target.

Tight-lipped, Clark turned into the manager's tent where he knew he would find Shreve himself.

CHAPTER TWO

TERROR RIDES HIGH

A S white as his snowy hair was the pallor of Henry Shreve's face. But his spiked mustache bristled and his jaw was set and he looked like what he was—a fighter. He seemed to be probing back of Bob Clark's steel-colored eyes for the thoughts which lay there, for Henry Shreve knew that Bob Clark would never expose his hand until finis had been written to the case.

Beside the carnival owner sat Fred Morgan, whose black hair shimmered under the gasoline light in the top of the tent. Morgan was Shreve's handyman—secretary, assistant manager, accountant. His light eyes were narrow now with fear, and his thick body was hunched in the chair.

"I never should have brought them," cried Morgan in a wailing voice. "I never should have brought them. I knew this would happen. They'll kill me, that's what they'll do. Kill me and cut me to pieces."

"Shut up," rapped Shreve, impatiently. He turned to Clark. "What's this all about?"

"The headhunters are loose," replied Clark, quietly. "Their grinder is lying up on their stage now without his head."

"Those are the facts," Shreve grated. "I know all that. I want your opinions!"

"All right," said Clark. "It amounts to just this. The murderer unlocked the manacles and let the headhunters loose. He was of medium height and had blond hair. He wore gloves."

Henry Shreve controlled his voice with an effort. "You mean that this has a tie-up with—you know."

"Sure it has. Furthermore, he wants me out of the way. Tried to kill me. Laid in wait outside the back of the tent. He's wise."

"You mean that," Morgan gasped, "that a white man—"

"Yes," said Clark, simply. "A white man is at the bottom of it someplace. Maybe the cannibals did the killing. Maybe not. But it wasn't their idea."

"Oh, God!" wailed Morgan. "I never wanted to go and get them. They're killers!"

"You were paid well to go to Nigeria after these fellows, and they've been worth a mint to us," Shreve broke in. "It's clear that someone doesn't want me to get along. Perhaps, Clark, you don't know that a reign of terror would drive away the crowds, and that a single week during which I couldn't make expenses would ruin me."

"You owe money?" asked Clark.

"I do."

"To whom?"

Shreve shrugged. "If you're thinking of that for a lead, you're wrong. A bank in New Jersey owns a first mortgage on the show. That bank has been closed as insolvent, and the receivers are disposing of the assets. But that, I believe, has little bearing on the case. This is a personal grudge. I've made plenty of enemies."

Jordson, head trainman of the show, loomed in the doorway, his face dark, his hands restless. Clark noted that Sven Jordson's hair was almost white.

"Mr. Shreve," growled the trainman, "I want my pay. I'm leaving, now, tonight."

Shreve leaned back in his chair. "Why?"

"I'm not staying around to get murdered. I want my pay."

Shreve's lips twitched with the ghost of a smile.

"You're sure this hasn't anything to do with the argument we had yesterday."

"No. Nothing." Jordson's face darkened.

"And you're sure you aren't trying to get even with me?"

"I don't know what you're talking about." Uneasily, the trainman shifted his weight, growling deep in his throat.

Clark stepped forward, his face expressionless, his movements slow.

"We're going to detain you, Jordson," he said quietly. "Maybe you'll want to confess."

The trainman's eyes shot wide. He took an involuntary step backwards and then, as swift as a bolt of lightning, he lashed out with a hamlike fist and caught Clark just below the ear. Clark snorted and stepped in, both hands lancing out with vicious speed.

Jordson's bulk reeled back. His arms blurred as he struck. His heavy shoes thudded on the tent platform. His lips were parted in a snarl. Clark's fists seemed to pound against granite.

The canvas vibrated under the shock of the lunging bodies. Shreve was half on his feet, mouth partly open with excitement. Morgan sat in his chair, eyes darting first to one, then to the

13

other, as though ready to spring out of the way should they weave too close to him.

Clark was fighting with the cool deliberation of the trained boxer, but Jordson depended on slow haymakers which were easily dodged. And then, quite unexpectedly, the trainman slid out to his length on the floor, unconscious.

Shreve jumped up with a terse, "Good work." He pulled a gun out of his desk and turned to Morgan. "Kick that squarehead awake and hustle him over to the train. Lock him up in a stateroom and put a husky at the door to guard him. Got it?"

"But—" stammered Morgan, his eyes suddenly wide. He made a wry face and shrugged. "All right."

A bucket of water brought the trainman back to life, and when Morgan had taken him away, Shreve sat down and smiled at Clark. "That was what I call fast work."

Clark shot his cuffs and grunted.

"Maybe," he said. "But even if he was the guy who set the headhunters free, the fact still remains that the headhunters are on the loose. Tell me. Why is Morgan so scared?"

Shreve leaned back.

"He had a right to be," he admitted. "He was the one that brought the headhunters over from Africa. We sent him on a special trip. You see, the Nigerian government frowns on the practice, and they had some of those little fellows in prison. To save themselves a prison bill, they let us have them cheap. Naturally the headhunters didn't like the arrangement, and they seem to have taken it out on the trip across by making life miserable for Morgan.

"He thinks they got loose just to get even with him. But I don't believe it. Those fellows haven't got any more sense than a pinhead, and their memories aren't that long."

"So far so good," Clark nodded. "But I don't think that that is the whole story. I came down here to locate a narcotics ring that was peddling dope along your right-of-way. You and I have looked every place in the show for possible hiding places for that dope, and we've tried like nailers to get next to the man who was doing the peddling. Somehow, some way, this thing ties up. I feel it.

"Three towns back, a politician was murdered. That connects up. What was his name? McDonald—that was it. Shot twice in the stomach. Before that, a teamster was found stabbed in the 'House of Horror,' or whatever they call it.

"Tonight a grinder is decapitated and a man tried to kill me. We're in for a reign of terror, all right. That crowd out there doesn't know it yet, and I hope they don't find out before you get enough dough to run you a while."

Henry Shreve's mustache bristled anew. He thrust out his jaw.

"I'm not licked yet." He paused, busy with his thoughts. "But see here, Clark. You aren't here to solve murders, and you're running too great a risk. I'm going to call in the State Police."

"No, you're not," rapped Clark. "They'd ruin my chances. I'm here on a job, and I'm going to do it, murder included.

Now that this ball has started rolling, it's going to keep up, and if I can't get on the bandwagon tonight I never can. As carnival detective, I have a free rein. The police will be here to take a hand soon enough, Shreve."

The owner of the show started to reply, but a sudden bedlam of cries out in the midway drowned whatever words he had uttered. He started up in alarm as the volume of sound grew.

Bob Clark sprang for the door and lanced through. The blaze of lights which marked the main avenue of the carnival fell upon the motley crowd where they drew back and bunched together.

In spite of the press of bodies, Clark fought his way through until he stood in front of the largest concession on the lot, a building which was dubbed "The House of Horror." It was there that the cries were the loudest.

People were pressing back away from something, and people in the outer ring were pushing forward, trying to see, spurred by curiosity.

Clark saw a space in the center of the midway opening up. He saw women hiding their faces and men staring with terror-glazed eyes.

He mounted the steps of a ticket booth and looked down.

There on the dusty, trampled grass, lids open in a sightless stare, lay the head. Clark swore to himself when he recognized it. It was the head of the murdered barker.

The hideousness of the thing was increased by the bluish spotlights which glared down at it from poles. It lay as though dropped from the sky.

There on the dusty, trampled grass,
lids open in a sightless stare,
lay the head.

Panic had begun to clutch at the crowd. They remembered, now, the scream. They remembered the vague rumors of murder. Many began to sweep down toward the exit, but more were held on the grounds by morbid curiosity.

All concessions were at a standstill, though the merry-go-round organ blared stridently on with its blatant music.

A tarpaulin lay at hand and Clark scooped it up. He fought his way to the cleared spot, and with a swift cast, he flung it over the head. Gingerly, without touching it, he wrapped the canvas about it and strode toward the nearest fringe of the crowd. They fell away from him, white-faced and shaking.

In Shreve's tent, Clark laid his gruesome burden, still wrapped, on a chair and turned to go out again. Then he saw Shreve lumbering toward him.

"Jordson got away!" bellowed Shreve. "He knocked out Morgan and took the gun and beat it."

Without a trace of emotion Clark walked swiftly beside Shreve back to the spot where Morgan lay, face down, in the dust.

Fred Morgan's temple was dark with blood. His hands clutched at the dirt convulsively. Shreve and Clark picked him up and carried him back to the tent office, where they laid him on the floor.

When they had brought him back to consciousness, he was in a panic and his voice was tight with fear.

"He's got a gun, I tell you," he chattered. "They'll kill all of us now. He turned on me and laughed and took that revolver as though I was made of straw. He almost killed me!"

18

"Calm down," said Clark, a little disgusted. "He isn't interested in killing you."

"You didn't see his face!" wailed Morgan. "He picked me up like a sack of straw and shook me and said he was going to kill all of us. He's got those four devils working for him."

After that outburst, Shreve's handyman subsided and turned his face away from them. Nervously he twisted his hands. Finally, he drew himself up into a chair and sat there staring vacantly off into space with unseeing eyes.

Coldly, Clark appraised him. Now that the showman veneer was gone, Morgan was showing himself to be yellow. Everything about him was tawdry, from his sleek black hair to the enormous square ring he affected.

"You stay here," said Clark, stepping to the door. "You've got another gun, Shreve, and I don't think you're in any danger. I've got to find Jordson or whoever it was that threw this into the midway."

"Threw what?" asked Shreve.

For answer, Clark lifted the side of the canvas and displayed the revolting severed head.

"The man who was killed tonight," he said tersely.

Shreve gasped and there was a shrill cry, followed by a dull bump. With a grimace of distaste, Clark saw that Morgan had passed out.

19

CHAPTER THREE

DEATH IN THE CRYSTAL

FOR an instant, Bob Clark stood staring out at the crowd which babbled its excitement. Though much thinner, the ranks of the pleasure-seekers still filled the midway.

Grifters were making a half-hearted attempt to run their gambling games. The Ferris wheel was still spinning, filling the night with its whirling glare. The merry-go-round still wheezed its honky-tonk music.

And then Bob Clark started violently. Out there he had caught sight of a face. Blond hair straggling out from under a slouch cap. A pinched face. Fear-ridden eyes. The face he had seen back of the headhunter sideshow!

The detective darted out, vaulting stakes and elbowing his way through the crowd. He still caught an occasional glimpse of the cap, and leaving semidestruction in his wake, he followed it.

For a brief instant the young face was turned in his direction and then hurriedly turned away. Clark's quarry broke into a run which was impeded by stands and people. Clark followed grimly.

The cap bobbed on its erratic course. Around trucks, past tents, through tight huddles of men, now running, now walking swiftly.

Ahead lay a row of tents—the freaks. Banner after banner floating under the blue white glare of spots.

The Spider Woman. The Armless Wonder. The Dog-faced Boy. Major Midget. And there, almost in the center, that ugly splash of color—headhunters squatting beside their victim—beneath which a murder had lately been done.

But the face under the cap took no notice of these. He seemed to veer toward a tent which was stamped with a phrenologist's chart, a gigantic palm profusely lined, and a crystal. Red letters a foot high proclaimed the presence of Madame Estrella, clairvoyant.

Ballyhooing grinders were getting back into their raucous stride. The glaring night was filled with the carnival turmoil. But Clark had eyes only for the cap.

Suddenly he lost sight of his quarry. He stopped for a moment to ascertain whether or not his man would again appear, and then, convinced of his destination, Clark elbowed his way toward Madame Estrella's.

He stopped before the door and peered intently into the dim interior, but only a tawdry screen rewarded his scrutiny. Boldly he stooped and entered and, finding no one in the outer canvas room, he pushed his way through a set of drapes and found himself standing before the reading table which held a crystal ball.

For the briefest of instants, Bob Clark forgot why he had come. The reason was sitting easily in a large, overstuffed chair, regarding him with a cool, impersonal gaze.

The girl was veiled to the eyes, but those were deep and liquid brown. Even the blue veil and the gaudy gypsy clothes could not hide the girl's beauty. Although she barely moved, she gave the impression of uncoiling.

"You wish to have your fortune told?" she asked in a rich voice.

Clark glanced about the room, noting that it was heavily draped. He could feel a tension here that was electric and crackling.

Two courses were open to him. He could search the place, battering down opposition, or convinced as he was that his man was in the room, he could seat himself and play a waiting game, hoping thereby to learn more than he would otherwise.

He could not remember having seen this girl before, though he knew that she had not been long with the show. Carefully weighing values in the split second allowed him, Clark smiled.

"Yes," he said. "I want to know the future very badly."

Languidly she waved toward a chair on the other side of the crystal ball. "You want me to read the crystal?"

Nodding, Clark sat down, every nerve tight with suspense.

"Your name," intoned Madame Estrella, "is Clark. You are engaged in very dangerous business."

She shaded her eyes and looked deep into the ball. Clark glanced at it and saw his own reflection.

Giving him a searching glance, she again dropped her eyes to the sphere.

"Your business will not be successful as you are combating forces which will not be denied," her voice droned on.

Clark looked at her narrowly. Was she warning him or threatening him?

"Your danger is great," she continued, almost tonelessly.

23

"If you do not drop the business at hand, your enemies will not stop at bringing about your death."

His lips twitched slightly. So she was threatening after all.

"What's the game, sister?" he rapped abruptly.

Her head jerked up, and through the veil he could see that she smiled. A sixth sense made him flash a glance at the crystal. Reflected there he saw a man behind him who held an upraised bludgeon in his hand. The weapon was coming down.

The image had no more than been transmitted to his brain when Clark moved. He weaved to one side like a shifting quarterback. Something crashed into his upper arm, numbing it.

Clark spun about, crouching. Above him and to the side was the pinched face he had followed. The eyes were dilated with the effort of the blow. The lips were drawn back tight over the teeth. The blond hair straggled over the forehead.

Clark struck up and knocked the youth away. Hurling himself forward with all the fury of a hurricane, Clark smashed the face with a dozen rapid blows. Behind him the girl cried out as though she herself had been struck.

"Blast you!" snarled the other. "You'll never take me. You'll never—" He raised the club up high and brought it down on Clark's shoulder.

Reeling, the detective caught at the table and slid down to the floor. As he fell, he snapped out with his good arm and encircled the other's legs, dragging the fellow down with him.

Dust billowed up from the rug. Draperies slithered down into tawdry heaps. The table teetered for an instant and then crashed over, taking the crystal with it. Clark caught a blurred glimpse of the girl standing back, her hands pressed frantically to her throat.

"The light!" sobbed Clark's assailant. "For . . . God's . . . sake . . . the light!"

Clark's fingers fought away the clawing nails which tore at his windpipe. Freed of that for an instant, he struck up at the face with a short, straight jab. The youth jerked almost to his feet and tottered there, collapsing like an empty sack. The detective lunged forward.

Then the tent was plunged into darkness. Clark snatched at empty air, reaching frantically about him. But the other was no longer on the floor.

Staggering upright, Clark flailed the air at random. His eyes were becoming accustomed to the gloom. Through the canvas walls, the glare of spots reached dimly.

A shadow moved across the room, slowly and silently. Clark leaped at it and missed. The shadow moved once more, and the detective stepped silently around to intercept it.

His arm shot out, and he felt cloth in his fingers. Tightening his grip, he jerked hard, bringing the shadow close to him. He expected a struggle, but, to his surprise, there was none.

Suddenly suspicious, Clark slipped to one side without changing the pressure of his grasp. The move saved his life. The tent flared blue with powder flame. Sparks stretched out like ribbons. The room was drowned with the explosion.

Angrily, Clark struck at the gun and knocked it across the room.

"You murdering hound!" he snapped.

And then the sleeve that he held grew taut and the shadow before him sank down to the floor. A muffled sob came to him from the rug. Scowling, Clark found his matches, struck one and applied it to the lamp.

When the wick of the gasoline lantern burned evenly, Clark set a chair upright and sat down. The girl on the floor, crumpled and tear-stained, sat very still and looked up at him.

"Why did you try to kill me?" said Clark, softly, once more the complete master of his emotions.

"You won't get anything out of me," choked Madame Estrella. Her veil was gone and Clark saw that her lips trembled.

"You wanted him to get away," Clark stated, evenly. "Why are you mixed up in this rotten game?"

"I'm not talking."

Clark shrugged. "But you will. I'm sending for the State Police as soon as we get out of here, and you happen to be close to going to the penitentiary for quite a stretch."

"Why tell me that?"

"Because I don't think you know what you are doing or what you have just done. That was attempted murder. You have harbored a criminal. And there are other charges which might be brought against you. If you cared to talk—"

"I'm not talking. But he isn't a criminal, and I wish I had killed you. It would have saved him the trouble."

"Meaning?"

The girl's voice was stronger and her head was held high. She got slowly to her feet.

"I mean that if you do not stop your persistence, Jack will kill you," she said firmly.

"So that's his name, eh? Jack what?"

"Don't pretend you don't know. What are you going to do?"

"I'm going to take you over to the train and have you locked up until you decide to talk." There was a quiet hardness to Clark's voice which bit deep.

Madame Estrella's was brittle and defiant.

"You will never reach the train with me," she said confidently. "Jack is out there now. I know that he is."

"Fine," smiled Clark. "Then we'll go get him. Perhaps he is a better conversationalist than yourself."

Pocketing the small-caliber gun he had knocked out of her hand, Clark led the girl to the door. She went without any great show of resistance, disdainfully confident that she would be delivered from her fate.

Clark strode out into the midway. There had been no excitement over the shot due to the nearness of a shooting gallery in which shots were constantly resounding.

The crowd was thinner and quieter. Few women remained. The barkers were reciting their spiels as of old, but their faces bore a strained look. Few were the people who paid them either attention or money.

The route to the sidetracked train lay straight down the midway. In front of the House of Horror stood a larger crowd than elsewhere, perhaps because those who remained at Shreve's Mammoth Carnival were held there only through a morbid interest in the events of the night. The banners above this dubious palace of entertainment certainly fitted the character of the night.

It was common knowledge now that the headhunters had escaped. As he passed through the crowd, Clark could gather that much from conversational scraps. He wondered that the menace was not sufficient to drive everyone off the grounds.

Madame Estrella had replaced her veil. She seemed indifferent to the stares directed at her, though her eyes occasionally darted to either side searchingly.

When they were still a hundred feet away from the entrance to the House of Horror, Clark sensed that something was wrong. Wide-eyed men were backing away, their movement suddenly panicky.

And then, for the second time that night, the glare was split apart by a scream of terror.

CHAPTER FOUR

The Headhunters

L IKE a tide, the crowd scuttled back, running, sweeping across the midway. They caught Clark and the girl in the sheer press of numbers and carried them back several steps before Clark secured sufficient footing to hold his ground.

In trying to surge forward against the wave, he lost the girl, and when he glanced back for her she had been swallowed up in the panic. He realized that any hope of trying to find her in the surging mob was futile—and a wave of disappointment swept over him. He had hoped to learn a great deal from the girl.

But Clark hesitated only for the briefest instant. No sounds came from the House of Horror now. But the silence bespoke a grisly discovery which Clark knew he would make there.

Overhead the banners fluttered drearily, depicting coffins, skeletons and, quite correctly, murder. They proclaimed an assortment of sights, thrills, sensations, not the least of which was the Mirror Maze.

Reaching the steps at last, Clark scrambled up to the platform and hurled himself through the door, recoiling as he saw the hideous thing which still twitched on the floor.

Lying there in a red lake was a headless body. The ripped clothing was of extreme cut and pattern, proclaiming that the owner had lately been a barker.

Clark remembered the man. A yellowish face, uneven teeth, a harsh, word-worn voice, shifty, colorless eyes. But whoever or whatever he had been, Clark felt that not even such as he could possibly merit so savage a death.

Thrusting his own compunctions aside, Clark rolled the body over. He pulled the red and dripping shirt away from the smeared chest, and stared for a long moment.

Blood still poured from a peculiar wound over the barker's heart. Using the silk handkerchief in the dead man's breast pocket, Clark cleared the wound for inspection.

Two incisions were there, not unlike the marks made by the fangs of a snake. Clark frowned slightly and brought himself to measure the depth of the cuts.

A little startled, he saw that the gashes were less than an inch deep, which meant that the implement had been less than three-quarters of an inch long, due to flesh compression under a blow.

He looked in the clenched hands for blond hairs, but found none. After a brief scrutiny of the stained planks, Clark stood up, narrow-eyed and frowning.

Footsteps behind him caused him to turn. Shreve and Morgan were coming up, hesitant at the sight of the corpse. Morgan's mouth was twitching at the sides with terror.

"The headhunters," growled Shreve.

"Maybe," Clark admitted. "And again, maybe not."

"I'll be next," said Morgan with dead certainty. "They won't stop until they get me."

He twisted his hands together, the light jumping from his foppish rings. He stared about him blankly.

Clark grunted.

"Get two huskies and have them stay with Morgan, Shreve," he directed. "No use of anything happening to him. Take him over to your private car and see to it that nobody gets to him. If anyone tries, have him arrested. Get it?"

"Thank God!" croaked Morgan, seeming to breathe easier. "Aren't you ever going to send for the State bulls?"

"I'm sending for them now. Call them, will you, Shreve? I think I've let this thing go far enough. There'll be more murders before this thing is through and people are liable to ask too many questions if we slip up on calling the police."

No other man on the grounds would have dared to so order Henry Shreve about. But he took it without protest.

"What are you going to do?" he asked quietly.

Clark shrugged.

"I've got an idea that those four headhunters won't be far away, and I'm going to try and find some trace of them. There's probably one or two other men mixed up in this and I've a fair idea who they are. I'm going to try to get the works in one fell swoop."

"I'll send a couple stake men with you," stated Shreve.

"Don't want them. Bullets will fly, and I make less of a target than three men would. I'm going to start out by searching through this place."

"Alone?" Morgan blurted.

"Alone," said Clark, patting the bulge in his coat under which lay a gun.

He pulled his gray felt hat down over his forehead and walked toward the shadowy aisle ahead.

The House of Horror consisted of demountable plank sides and occasional squares of canvas. It was large for a transportable building, and, in the estimation of Clark, made the only good hideaway on the carnival grounds.

He came to the first room, which glowed under sickly blue lights. Two papier-mâché skeletons sat at a table playing cards, caps drawn jauntily over gaping eyes, bony fingers clasped tightly over whiskey glasses, cigarettes dangling from yellow teeth.

They grinned ghoulishly at each other, so realistic that one half-expected to see them move. The pointed moral of the tableau was that indulgence in drinking, gambling and smoking would bring about an early death.

Clark permitted himself a twisted grin and walked through to the next room. Here a coffin lay among artificial flowers, and when Clark stepped over the door jamb, the corpse sat up straight and turned its head in his direction.

The detective started violently and stepped back. With a creak, the wax figure sank back into the box. Suddenly Clark realized that he had stepped upon a floor plate which had caused the action. He railed mildly at himself for his sudden case of nerves and walked on.

The carnival was quieting down. The merry-go-round no longer blazed away and the Ferris wheel no longer whirled. Grifters were closing up their stands and drifting back to their quarters on the train. It was in this seemingly unnatural quiet that Clark heard a footstep just ahead of him.

He pressed himself against the side of the wall, watchful, wondering who might be there. His fingers rested on his gun butt. The footsteps, cautious and shuffling, came to him again. Leaning slightly forward, Clark gazed down the bend in the passageway.

Clark's eyes suddenly blazed with interest. Not twenty feet away from him, the blond youth was creeping along with his back in Clark's direction.

The detective's first impulse was to snap down on the man called Jack, but he stayed it, deeming it wiser to wait until Jack reached his destination. Something told Clark that the headhunters were not far away.

Oblivious of his observer, the man called Jack worked forward as silently as he could across the rough planks.

Ahead was another turn in the passage, and the blond youth worked toward it. Suddenly his movements were no longer slow. He dived around the corner, and there his footsteps seemed to stop.

Eyes alight with eagerness, Clark ran on the balls of his feet until he was at the bend. Sliding silently down the wall, he glanced up the dim passage. His mouth twitched. The man called Jack was not in sight.

It was only with an effort that Clark kept himself from running forward. His quarry might be waiting for him in ambush. Nevertheless, the detective's short, quiet walk brought him into another room in a surprisingly short space of time.

He glanced about him, noting that this display was termed a medical museum and that the place was lined with alcohol pots which held gruesome exhibits. But of the man called Jack there was neither sight nor sound.

Clark noticed that another passageway seemed to double

back toward the entrance. Afraid that his man had seen him and was making good another escape, the detective plunged recklessly forward.

In the third room he crossed, something intangible stayed his rush. He pressed himself against the wall and gazed intently ahead.

From behind a cabinet came the white face of his quarry. The eyes shot wide with fear. The man called Jack catapulted himself out into the room and rushed heedlessly down a passage in full view of the detective.

Clark tugged at his gun and then thought better of it. He couldn't shoot a man in the back. Weapon in hand, he sprinted forward in hot pursuit.

Another turn in the alleylike passage led out to two possible ways of escape. One was to the outside, and the other doubled back over the trail which Clark had just completed. Knowing that even a fear-crazed man would know better than to run across the almost deserted grounds in the full glare of spots, Clark chose the other course.

Though he traveled swiftly, he was cautious. If the man called Jack was still in the building, he would be waiting at some hidden turn, ready to club or shoot the detective down.

In the room with the skeletons, hurrying though he was, Clark's practiced eye saw that one of the whiskey glasses had been knocked out of a bony hand. His quarry had passed there and had accidentally hit the skeleton.

The detective darted into the next room, which held the wax corpse. He stepped across the door jamb, gave the motionless casket contents a brief glance and then slipped out into the corridor, forging ahead. He increased his speed and his caution, but he did not again catch sight of the blond-headed youth.

Suddenly Clark stopped and swore at himself. Not until now did he realize that the wax dummy had not risen up when he stepped upon the plate. Bitterly, he knew that his quarry had hidden himself in that coffin.

Retracing his steps at a run, Clark stopped beside the crude box and looked down. It was empty. In a heap in the corner lay the wax figure, braces and springs dragging forlornly.

But Clark did not bother to follow. He had been pursuing his man for many minutes, and several had elapsed since he had passed through this room the second time. The man called Jack had had ample time to cross the midway into the shelter of trucks and baggage.

Clark stood no chance of finding him now. He could only go ahead with his investigation of the House of Horror. Even though he supposed the other gone, Clark went ahead carefully. There were others in this structure. Of that he was sure.

The passage of a few minutes brought him to still another section of the place. This was the Mirror Maze in which so many customers had been so joyfully lost. To all appearances, it was deserted now.

Confident of his own ability to find his way through, the detective stepped into the narrow aisle to be flanked immediately by dozens of Clarks which were in profile, facing him, with their backs to him. The sensation made him a little dizzy, and his nerves felt slightly raw.

35

He walked forward, bumping into plain glass here and there. Often dodging at his own reflection, feeling like a perfect fool the instant he had done so. The place was a crystal labyrinth, appearing far more vast than it actually was. But Clark felt certain that he had hit upon the one place in the grounds where men could be concealed without seeming to be.

The passageway, glittering and filled with his own image, twisted and turned endlessly. Every few seconds, Clark pressed his ear against a mirror to listen. Once he thought he caught the sound of rustling cloth, but he was not sure.

Then the whisper came again, faintly. Clark darted into a V turn and glanced down both aisles. Suddenly he saw a movement which could not be his own because he was standing very still.

A head and a pair of shoulders jutted out into the passage and then caught sight of the detective's reflections. It was gone as soon as it had come.

But in that brief space of time Clark had noted three characteristics of the man. His face was puffy, his hair was straw white, and he wore a slouch cap.

Clark's mind whirled with speculations. Was it Sven Jordson? Was it the blond youth? No, he did not feel that it was either of those, although it might have been.

There was something extremely familiar about that gesture of looking out. Something hauntingly familiar about it. Clark recalled that the knife-thrower had straw white hair. Could it have been he?

Clark had stood there for a matter of seconds, waiting, gun in hand, when he caught sight of another movement in the mirrors. Flame spurted out, a horizontal column of sparks. The bullet passed within a foot of Clark's head, showering him with glass from the shattered mirror.

Clark's own gun belched lead, making the structure vibrate with the thunder of the shot. But the instant he fired he knew that his target had only been an image. He was suddenly maddened by his inability to distinguish the real from the unreal. He fired a second time and struck another mirror.

After that he waited in a crouch, feeling that death was not far away from him. The watch on his wrist ticked regularly, the only sound in the crystal maze. And still he waited.

At last he heard a low mutter, which seemed to come from the back of the glass. Feeling certain that his late assailant had departed to wait for better hunting, Clark worked his way along toward one of the mirrors which had been broken by his own shots.

The mutter seemed to grow in volume. An odor floated to him, heavy and depressing, the smell of unwashed bodies. Feeling exposed on all sides, accompanied by his own position-twisted images, Clark slowly made his way until he could see through the large hole. Most of the glass had been smashed out of the frame, due to the glancing blow struck by the lead.

The mutter was no longer audible. Clark pressed his face closer to the opening. But the other side seemed dark and empty. No planks there. Dried grass filled the bottom of the apparent pit.

As this was still part of the House of Horror, Clark was at a loss to account for the waste of so much space. He felt

The bullet passed within a foot of Clark's head, showering him with glass from the shattered mirror.

that he was on the verge of making an extremely important discovery.

Hearing nothing more, Clark shifted his gun to his left hand and dropped through the split panel. The ground was three feet down, and he groped for it with his feet, carefully avoiding cuts from the shattered glass.

He loosed his hold and stood upright, blinking in the gloom. His eyes accustomed themselves to the dimness gradually, and Clark was about to move on when he caught sight of a shadow. Someone was near him. More than one.

He jerked up his gun and clamped down on the butt. But in that instant, the gun was sent spinning away from his hand and he was attacked on three sides at the same time.

First he saw teeth, filed and bared in a snarl. Then he saw the white of dark eyes. Steel flashed through the dark, and Clark felt a point pressing itself against his throat.

He kicked out savagely and twisted about, but the hold on his arms tightened and the knife point pricked his skin. Suddenly afraid that he might cut his own gullet by a quick movement, Clark forced himself to remain quiet.

CHAPTER FIVE

MYSTERY OF THE KNIVES

J ABBERING gutturally, the headhunters growled at one
another, still holding their captive at the knife point, as
though they were undecided as to the best course of disposal.
Their eyes seemed to glow redly, and their filed teeth glinted.

Clark could see them better now, although his head was
held back and high. He was six inches taller than any of them,
but their strength, after so much inactivity in the pit, seemed
phenomenal. Their brown fingers were steel bands which
sunk viselike into the detective's muscles.

The needlelike point of the knife sunk a little deeper with
each passing second, but the headhunter who held it seemed
oblivious of the pressure. Pain coursed sharply and achingly
through Clark's throat and jaw muscles.

His back was flat to the platform edge, and each time the
detective moved the smallest fraction of an inch, the pressure
on the blade increased.

Still the headhunters babbled in low tones. The one who
clasped the hilt seemed to be their leader. He talked more
harshly and authoritatively. But, evidently, the other three
did not agree with his decision, for they dissented with vigor.

Clark remembered attending their show days before. They
had sat listlessly in their pit, glaring sullenly up at the curious

while their ballyhoo man, who was now dead and headless in their tent, ran off his spiel.

They lived on half-cooked flesh, the barker had said, and considered a human heart the greatest delicacy. They hunted heads for several reasons.

They were supposed to practice cannibalism whenever possible, but this was not the actual cause of their headhunting. Some way they thought the head possessed fertility, and each crop-sowing season they must fare forth in search of victims. If they did not, their crops would not grow properly.

Clark wondered dully what they could want with him. They did not, could not understand that he was a detective who would restore them to captivity. He was only another white man who had disturbed them in their retreat. They did not know him personally as they must have known their own spieler and the barker of the House of Horror.

Then, greatly to Clark's surprise, the pressure on the knife began to lessen gradually. It drew slowly away from his throat until it no longer touched his skin. Soon a foot of dim space intervened, and the detective was not long in taking advantage of the fact.

He darted to one side, wrenching himself away from the clutching hands. Taken unaware, the headhunters released all grips for new holds and thereby lost out entirely. Clark dodged under their arms and shot across the room to where his gun lay glinting.

With a swift scoop, he touched the butt of the weapon, but a bare brown foot was quicker. Once more the weapon shot away from him, and he darted for it.

But hands had caught him again, and he twisted violently against the savage embraces. A ragged pain shot through his thigh, and he knew the knife had gone home. With renewed energy, he reached out for a hand which held another blade aloft.

He snatched the long hilt and turned it. The edge bit into the headhunter's hand, and he released it with a howl.

Another hand shot up and grasped the point with a vicious jerk. Clark held fast, and even though the glimpse was brief, he found time to be surprised at what happened. The knife broke in two pieces! A headhunter had the blade and Clark had the hilt.

A two-by-four section slashed into play, wielded by the leader of the four. He stood back, calmly plying his bludgeon whenever any section of Clark's head and shoulders was displayed.

The detective tried to escape the scientific application of the murderous timber, but he was unsuccessful. Dimly he knew that he was sinking into unconsciousness.

He clutched at the knife hilt and tried desperately to bring it down on the hard, woolly skulls.

Then he forgot where he was and what he did. Blackness that was unreal and suffocating swarmed over him and dragged him down. He sprawled at length on the floor, covered with dust and spattered blood, completely at the dubious mercy of his captors.

Bob Clark did not know how long he had been out, but he did know that he was lying flat on his back and that his arms and legs were tied painfully tight. He lay still, waiting for full possession of his senses, grateful for a current of air which ran along the ground and cooled the fever in his face.

He was aware of the headhunters about him, though they were silent now. He knew that the carnival was almost wholly closed down by this time, for he could hear no sounds out on the midway.

Perhaps the State Police would arrive before anything happened to him, and again, perhaps Shreve had never reached his office tent after leaving the House of Horror. Or, more likely, the white man who was at the bottom of this would come back and put an end to him.

Clark fell to speculating upon the identity of the man who had shot at him. The more he thought about it, the dimmer grew the image in his mind. He finally decided that the blond youth called Jack had been the one.

After a long interval he became conscious of a cylinder in his hand. His arms were tied in an X across his chest, and by dint of much straining he could finally view the round, heavy thing he held. It was hollow and made of a dull metal.

Then he remembered grasping the hilt of the knife, and how the weapon had come apart. But why were the handles detachable? And why was there a cavity there?

The answer made him forget that he ached and that he was tired. This knife was of a type commonly employed by blade-throwers. He recalled the unseemly number of them which had been piled in the knife-thrower's stand, and how careful the man had been to use only certain ones in his act.

Clark had been searching for this thing for months, and now here it was resting figuratively within his grasp. This was the storage space of the narcotics which had radiated out from the carnival. A small fortune could have been concealed in that pile he had seen.

Straining anew, he brought his nose close to the hollow and sniffed at it. There were no doubts in his mind now. Cocaine had been lately contained in that hilt!

He had guessed at this tie-up from the first. Whoever was in back of the dope smuggling also wanted to see Shreve's Mammoth Carnival go out of business. They had freed the headhunters to bring about a reign of terror, scattering the carnival to the four winds. Perhaps they had thought their trail too broad and that this was the easiest way to cover it up.

But that girl. Where did she fit in? And the blond youth called Jack. Why had that politician, McDonald, been shot, and why had Sven Jordson fought him? Did the teamster's death connect up with this at all?

Clark knew that if he didn't get loose and solve this, Shreve would soon be without his show, Morgan would collapse with fear, and Clark's own standing would be ruined with the Department. After all, how many times had his immediate superior said, "It's a dumb dick that gets himself killed." Clark didn't want to be either dumb or dead.

In his determination, Bob Clark gripped hard on the cylinder the headhunters had failed to take away from him. It cut the edge of his thumb and he almost dropped it.

When he gripped it again, he did not care whether it cut him or not. Still, even if he got free, he would be allowed short shrift at the hands of these ugly devils who were hunched together in the corner of the cramped interior.

Then from somewhere above and outside, a voice floated faintly to him. Clark stiffened. It was that of the girl, Madame Estrella.

"—before long—" came the few distinct words in the murmur.

"—kill him. It's the only thing we can do." A deeper tone indicated that a man spoke.

The girl answered him in a tone which was almost hysterical. "They've called in the police. And when they come it will be too late. We can't stay here then. They'll know and they'll find out all about it. Kill him the first chance you get.

"I don't care how!" she cried after a pause. "Kill him. It's all we can do. When they find out about—" Her voice dropped. "Cocaine and— Nobody will miss him— They'll think those headhunters did it."

A long silence followed, and Clark's mind whirled. But he did not lose this chance to work. The headhunters were looking up towards the sound, and Clark could see their eyes.

He thrust the sharp edge of the hilt rim against the cord which bound his arms and began to saw vigorously, though silently. He ached with effort, for he knew too well that failure would cost him his head.

The headhunters had turned back now, and the detective was forced momentarily to discontinue his bid for liberty. His steel-colored eyes stared blankly up at the canvas top.

Suddenly a gasp of pain lanced through the wall. Feet pounded, and the swift smacks of knuckles against flesh and bone echoed through the darkness. An occasional grunt, the sharp intake of breath, finally a wail of pain, and the fight evidently was done.

Twice after that there were the sounds of a sharp scuffle, but each time they subsided.

"You'll never get away with this," Clark heard the girl say. "I'll—"

There the sound was cut off and muffled as though someone had clapped a hand over the girl's mouth.

During the fight, Clark had worked hard. The hilt rim was dull at best, but the hemp which held his arms was old and soft, and it finally began to come away. At first he could move only his forearm, and then he could shift both hands. He did not know as yet just how he would get past the vigilance of his captors.

On the other side of the sectional partition, Clark heard a hinge creak, and then the sound of a body being dragged over the dusty ground. A man grunted with effort and then called out something in a staccato jabber which brought the headhunters to their feet as one man. They looked at one another, said a few words, and then looked fearfully toward the partition.

The unseen man spoke again, harshly, loud. The headhunters moved quickly toward a loose board and removed it. One by one they passed out of the enclosure, leaving Clark alone.

That was all the detective wanted. With a mighty heave of his arms, he parted the few remaining strands of rope and then bent over quickly to undo his feet. His movements were stiff and fumbling, due to the ache of his muscles. But the task required only an instant.

Clark stood up and groped for the broken mirror. It was darker now, and he could not see well. Unexpectedly, his foot cracked into the two-by-four of his former experience and he tripped headlong, saved only by snatching at the edge of the glass frame.

A loud oath came from the other room, followed immediately by the scurry of feet. The loose board crashed aside. Clark had swung himself almost all the way up to the raised platform which served as a runway for the Mirror Maze. He felt a hand grip his trouser leg, but he knocked it aside.

With every ounce of his strength brought to bear, Clark flung himself at length on the planks and then scrambled to his feet. His assailant was coming up through the hole after him.

Clark smashed a blow into the face and raced away. He could hear the slump of the body behind him, and he smiled to himself, secure in the knowledge that finally he was free.

CHAPTER SIX

The Death of Morgan

O UTSIDE, the midway was lit only by a few sparse electric bulbs. Only the carnival crowd was there, eating their past-midnight supper at the grease joint. But tonight, laughter was scarce.

Two of their number had been struck down in a horrible way, and it was only a trouperlike attachment to the show which kept them on the grounds at all. Many of them had gone back to the train a short distance away to pass the night in fitful, nightmare-rent slumber.

They stared at Bob Clark as he passed and waved him a hesitant greeting. And well they might stare. For Clark's ordinarily neat appearance was gone, and in its place walked a scarcely recognizable scarecrow, covered with dust and dried blood.

He was heading back to Shreve and Morgan's private car, where he had sent the latter earlier that night. Apprehension for the safety of Shreve speeded his tired feet.

While he was still a hundred feet away from the orange-colored car, he knew that something was wrong. He could see the crumpled form of a man on the platform near the steps.

Clark broke into a run and knelt quickly beside the man. It was, presumably, one of the men who had been sent to guard

Morgan. With a sigh of relief, the detective noted that the man still breathed. Dousing the face with water from a fire bucket, Clark brought him around.

The guard sat up unsteadily, shaking his head and coughing.

"What happened?" Clark demanded.

The guard gave him a careful scrutiny, sparring for time to regain the use of his tongue.

"I don't know," he said finally. "A bird jumped me from the roof of the car and we scrapped. That's all I remember." He got to his feet, still shaking his head. "Where's Billy?"

"Billy? Who's that?"

"The other guy that was supposed to watch with me here."

"I don't know," said Clark. "You better get up to your bunk and get some rest. You look pretty sick."

After the man had gone, Clark stepped up into the car. It was divided into two parts, a third of which belonged to Morgan and two-thirds to Shreve. It served as office and living quarters for the two.

But the usual tidiness of the place had been completely disrupted. As he had supposed, it was untenanted. A ghastly smear of blood, now partially clotted, lay in a pool on Morgan's green rug. The bunk was smeared red, as was the desk.

Overhead, a trapdoor in the roof gaped emptily at the sky. A chair was smashed to splinters, and the desk was out of place.

Clark stepped through the partition and discovered that Shreve's portion of the car was almost untouched, save for litter on the desk which gave evidence that someone had lately gone through the carnival owner's papers.

Back in Morgan's third, Clark jerked out several drawers

and scattered their contents out in front of him. He poked into the pigeonholes and dragged out disarrayed objects which had already been mishandled.

And then he discovered something. A small cluster of glass tubes came to light, each of them stoppered with sealing wax. Clark shrugged to himself and broke a seal, pouring the contained crystals out into his palm. He needed no chemical analysis to tell him that this was cocaine.

He stepped back and gave the desk a long stare.

"They weren't hard to find," he told himself. "Almost in plain sight. I wonder—"

Puzzled, he looked about him.

The glare of the lights caught and held a glistening something beside the edge of the carpet. He stooped down and lifted the green rug, uncovering a small pile of white metal filings. He picked up a long sliver and bit it.

"Silver," he decided.

But whatever other investigations he wanted to make were held up for the moment. Through the window he saw a stream of headlights coming across the track and toward the car, accompanied by the dying moan of a siren. The State Police had arrived.

The first man Clark met on the platform was Shreve. The older man came up panting, mustache bristling.

"I brought them, Clark, but I guess I was too late," he exclaimed.

A State Police captain loomed on Clark's right. "What were you doing in that car?" he snapped.

Clark smiled and motioned for the captain to follow

him back into the interior. They went, followed by Shreve. Strangely enough, neither of the newcomers seemed excited about the quantity of blood on the floor.

Bob Clark extracted a small gold disk from a pouch around his neck and, holding it in the flat of his hand, showed it to the captain.

"United States Secret Service," breathed the officer, a little awed. "I'm sorry, I—"

"It's all right," smiled Clark. "I didn't call you in before this because I thought I could make the pinch myself. But now I guess that's impossible."

"What do you mean?" boomed the captain.

"It looks like Morgan was the head of the narcotics ring which was operating out of this carnival. That's all I am here for. Looks odd, to find all this blood, but I guess Morgan had a fight and cleared out. Either that, or somebody wants to make it appear that he had."

"That last is right," the officer said with assurance. He turned to the door and called to the cars. "Boys, bring that thing up here."

Three troopers got down and lifted something out of the machine and brought it up the steps, depositing it on the green rug. It was a decapitated body.

"That blows my theory up," said Clark with a shrug. "Morgan was afraid he'd get it that way."

Shreve shook his head sadly.

"We found him out on the edge of the grounds, half in a swamp, just like he is," he said. "They didn't take his rings or his scarfpin."

"No," muttered Clark. "But they got his head. I'm right back where I started from now. This dope was just a plant, I guess."

He knelt beside the headless corpse and took hold of one of the hands.

"Morgan sure loved rings, didn't he?" remarked Clark. "But of all these diamonds, whoever killed him saw fit only to take that big square mosaic-looking thing he wore on his index finger."

"That's right," growled Shreve. "That ring is the only one that is gone. I wonder why they took that. It was the cheapest of the lot."

"Well, what I'm after," boomed the State Police captain, "are those four headhunters or whatever you call 'em. They've raised enough devil for one night. We've got to put a stop to this."

"Sure," Clark replied. "Round them up. But don't kill any of them."

"Why?" demanded the officer.

"Because they either didn't do anything or didn't know any better," stated Clark in a clear voice. He turned to Shreve. "Why did you leave Morgan here?"

"He was scared," Shreve defended. "He wouldn't go with me, and I thought he'd be safe enough. Somebody cut the telephone lines, and I knew I had better get the police personally."

Clark was suddenly drawn down to the dead hand once more. He lifted it and turned it over, and then he stood up, his eyes narrow.

"Round up your headhunters. I've got something to do."
And with that, Clark left them, his stride springy.

Bob Clark went back toward the House of Horror. He did
not expect to find anyone there, but he thought it would be
as good a place as any to start.

The wobbly structure of canvas and plank sections still had
a foreboding look, but Clark went around to the back to the
place where he thought the side trapdoor would be. If he was
absolutely right, he didn't need to go there, but he wanted to
be sure.

Silently he rounded a corner and stopped, every nerve
tense. Close beside the door stood a man in a slouch cap. It
was the youth called Jack.

Clark suddenly realized that he had forgotten to bring a
gun, so occupied had he been with his discovery. He could
only depend upon his fists, but at all costs he must capture
this man.

He lanced out of the shadow into full view. For a moment,
the other stood paralyzed with surprise and then turned to
run. He sped away like a whippet, though his course was erratic.

Clark raced after him. The grounds were clear now, and
there was little likelihood that his quarry could easily elude
him. However, there were shadows where a man might stop
and wait, and it was into one of these that the youth was
plunging.

Clark did not slacken his stride. He plunged into the
semidarkness and crashed into something which struck with
the rapidity of a snake.

Bracing himself against falling, Clark whirled and returned

the blows. He received two for every one he gave, for the other seemed crazed.

Suddenly the blond youth crooked an arm about Clark's throat and tried to squeeze down with a grip which threatened to snap the detective's spinal cord. Clark felt things going black. He kicked out with his heels and twisted violently, but the grip held tight.

Clark drove an elbow in a last effort. He caught his assailant in the stomach. There was a grunt. The hold slackened a fraction of an inch. Clark twisted away.

Unexpectedly the blond youth whirled about and ran. He streaked for the center of the midway as though blind to its lack of cover.

A shot crashed. Another shot. And then Clark knew that he was the target of an unseen gun. Without knowing the source of the firing, he could only baffle the ambusher's aim by running, and he took out after the man called Jack, not quite certain that it was not he who had done the firing.

In a matter of seconds they had passed the last stand and were pounding out into the darkness of the open plain. For a moment, Clark was afraid he had lost his man, but then he saw that the man called Jack was running slowly, haltingly, and he knew that the stomach blow was getting in its work.

Clark found a sudden spurt of speed left in his legs. He narrowed down the distance which remained between them, ready for the fight he expected to come.

But the youth suddenly stopped and faced about. His hands were open and empty at his sides. His breath was coming in wheezing gasps.

The detective advanced warily until only a few feet separated them. He expected flame to lash out at him or to be met with a sudden lunge. But in these he was doomed to disappointment.

"I'm finished," wheezed the other. "You can take me back. I'll go. Only . . . only for God's sake . . ." He stumbled, his eyes half-shut, talking only with great effort. "Only . . . help me find my sister!"

With that he pitched forward into the dust.

CHAPTER SEVEN

THE FUGITIVE

ENDLESS seemed the trip back to the train, for Bob Clark half carried the blond youth the entire distance. Most of the carnival people had departed from the grounds, but those who remained had witnessed the chase. However, they were no longer able to feel surprised.

Two troopers met Clark a short distance from the cars and helped him with his semiburden.

"That second coach," pointed Clark. "I've got a stateroom where I can talk to this fellow. I want you two to wait around outside in case I'm wrong in my judgment and anything happens."

They nodded and lifted the limp youth up to the platform and finally eased him to the transom. Respectfully, the troopers touched their hats in a half-salute and backed out. It was evident that they had never seen a Secret Service man before and did not quite know how to treat him.

Bob Clark rummaged around in a cupboard and pulled out a bottle of fine whiskey. Failing to find a corkscrew, he banged the cork out by slapping the heel of his hand against the base. Carefully, he poured out two strong drinks.

"I don't want that," said the youth, wearily.

"Take it and down it. What's your name?"

Obeying the command, the other gulped the drink, then coughed and made a face.

"Jack McDonald," he sputtered. "I thought you knew."

"I don't know what you thought I knew," replied Clark, not unkindly. "But I'd like to know a lot that you do."

He reached out and pulled a hair from McDonald's head.

Pulling an old envelope from his pocket, he extracted the five hairs he had taken from the hand of the dead barker. He opened a drawer and took out a small but powerful microscope and arranged the light. Silently he inspected the strands beneath the microscope.

Finally he put the instrument away and sat back on the edge of his bunk.

"It wasn't your hair, McDonald," he announced. "I'm fairly certain now that you didn't have anything to do with this beheading party someone is having tonight. I'm ready to believe anything you tell me."

"How can you tell?" asked the other, revived by the whiskey.

Clark drained his own glass. "Several ways. The man who is doing all this is several years older than you are, and he's had his head shaved in the last two or three years. It's coarse."

"Now," he continued, "what's the idea of all this tiptoeing around? And why did you have it in for me?"

McDonald seemed to slump. The freshened interest left his young face, and it was suddenly old.

"They'll know out there as soon as they get a good look at me," he muttered. "The State Troopers, I mean. There's a reward out for me."

"For what?"

"Murder," half-whispered the other. "I didn't do it. Honest I didn't. But my getting away made it look bad." He held up his chin with an effort. "You see, they accused me of murdering my father. I don't know how it happened, and I guess they think they have to have a goat and I was it."

"McDonald!" exclaimed Clark. "I get it now. McDonald was the politician who was shot a while ago."

"That was my father. He was pretty much the boss back in Marion. Everybody looked up to him, and they'd do anything he said."

"Sure," said Clark, wanting the boy to change the subject before he broke down again. "That was where a man was arrested peddling dope. I've got all that in my files."

"I better start at the beginning," said McDonald. "A man came up to the house one night and wanted to see Dad. I let him in. My sister and I were in the next room playing cribbage, and when I went back to the game, we could hear everything that was said.

"This fellow was pretty loud. His face was pretty thin, and he had a lot of fancy clothes on. I took him for a carnival man. His hair was straw white.

"He thought Dad had something to do with this dope peddler's arrest and he said that if Dad didn't get the man off, there'd be one less political boss in town. Dad told him to get out, and the fellow swore back at him pretty bad.

"I got up to go in, and just then I heard two shots, one right after the other. I swung the door open and saw this carnival man throw the gun at Dad's body and run out. I guess I must have gone sort of crazy. I picked up the gun and fired it at this carnival man twice.

"The neighbors came in and found me standing there beside my Dad—and, well, they arrested me because—I guess I'd wiped out all the fingerprints except my own." After a moment, McDonald went on. "They put me up for trial and found me guilty, and the next day they were going to move me to the State Penitentiary, where I was going to be electrocuted.

"Anyway, that night—I know you don't think it can be done, but we did it. My sister slipped me a file in a banana and a hacksaw in a loaf of bread. She'd read about it someplace. Anyway, I sawed my way out.

"We joined up with this carnival because we knew our man was here. My sister, Jean, knows palm reading. She used to do it for the charity bazaars. And so she's been keeping us eating with that, and I've been looking for our man. I've seen him several times. But tonight—"

McDonald's poise broke, and his head hung on his chest.

"Tonight Jean disappeared."

Suddenly something clicked in Clark's mind. He remembered that conversation he had overheard outside of the House of Horror between these two. Now he understood.

They had been talking about killing this white-headed murderer, not Clark. The girl had sent her brother away and had been taken prisoner during his absence.

Clark sprang to his feet and reached for a hat and gun.

"Come on," he cried. "I think we can find her. I just

remembered something about knives." He stopped for an instant and scrutinized McDonald's face. "Wait a minute. Where did you get that cut on your face?"

The youth put his hand up to his cheek, where two small incisions stood out redly against his pallor.

"That white-headed guy gave them to me," he remembered. "He just socked me. I met him—"

"Come on," exclaimed Clark, impatiently. "There's work to be done!"

Outside the two troopers fell in step with them. McDonald was slightly nervous in their presence, but his mind was almost wholly taken up with the possibility of his sister's and his own deliverance.

A few of the canvas-shrouded stands showed a fitful glimmer of light. But Clark stopped at none of these. He was not conducting a search. He knew where he was going, and he seemed to possess great certainty as to his success.

"We're going after a white-haired man," Clark told the troopers. "I'll show you where he is, presently, and I want you to stand outside in case he makes a break for it. But don't in any case shoot him fatally. Get that? He's worth nothing to us dead."

The troopers nodded, not at all averse to taking orders from a man who had a gold disk in his possession.

Ahead, a banner depicted the knife-throwing act, and from behind the platform there was a crack of light.

"This is the place," breathed Clark. "McDonald, you stay here with these fellows. Can't afford to have you shot up."

"But what are you going to do?" McDonald wanted to know.

"I'm going in and get him," said Clark in a matter-of-fact voice.

The troopers stood back, respectfully ready to do their part. Bob Clark unholstered his gun and walked straight up to the door of the tent. He did not pause for a moment in his stride when he threw open the door.

He was standing on the threshold of the dressing quarters, gazing into the dusty, trunk-strewn interior, but the occupants of the room were far too interested in their own affairs.

They stood facing one another, hands clenched at their sides, feet wide apart. The man with straw white hair was there and in his hand was a gun.

"You'll either take it on the lam," rasped the short, white-haired one, "or I'll kill you here and now."

"I'm up to your rotten game," snapped the knife-thrower. "You killed the other two because you were afraid they'd talk. And you're not going to kill me, get it?"

He flipped his hand and a knife appeared in it as though by magic.

"Hold it," said Clark, evenly, raising his gun. "There've been too many killings already."

Then the air between them flashed white with a streak of steel. Without an instant to spare, Clark ducked the knife. He shot from the hip and the man went down.

The other's gun bellowed. Clark darted to one side and shot again. He sent the gun hurtling away from the clutching hand, leaving a splotch of blood in its place.

With a shrill scream, the white-haired man dived for the door, murder in his eyes. Clark blocked the rush and threw him back. The other grasped at Clark's gun and brought it away with a dexterous flip quicker than the eye could follow. The gun described a short arc in the air, and a tongue of flame spat viciously at the detective's face.

Clark's knee curved up wickedly. His hands reached out with a swift one-two. He dived for the other's stomach and carried him back in a flying tackle.

Senseless, the white-haired man sprawled out on the floor.

The troopers appeared in the doorway, the light of battle in their eyes. Seeing that it was all over, they gave each other a disgruntled glance.

"Good work," said one.

But Clark had no time for compliments. He jumped to the center of the room and stared about the walls. Then he headed for a hanging drape and flung it back, revealing another room.

In this second tent room were five people. The four headhunters squatted on their heels, making no move. Clark saw that they were manacled once more. The fifth person was Madame Estrella, or, rather, Jean McDonald.

The girl's brother darted forward and quickly undid the confining knots. Without trying to understand what had taken place, the girl stood up stiffly.

The sound of a motor outside the tent grew louder and was then shut off. Three more troopers, their captain and Henry Shreve strode in.

"What's all the shooting about?" bellowed the captain.

"It's all over," stated Clark. "And I think I've got the works straightened out. You see that fellow just coming to on the floor? Well, gentlemen, I have a bit of a surprise for you—that is alias Fred Morgan."

CHAPTER EIGHT

THE WHITE-HAIRED MAN

GREAT amazement greeted the detective's decisive statement. For an instant the other men stared at him.

"Impossible," said Shreve indignantly. "Fred Morgan is dead!"

"You mean Billy Logan, one of the guards, is dead," corrected Clark. "And his headless body was arranged so we would think it was Morgan—who did it himself!"

"You're crazy," snapped Shreve. "I won't let you pin this on Morgan. He's dead, I tell you. Besides, even if he wasn't, I'm sure he couldn't possibly do such a thing.

"Why, Fred Morgan was my best friend. I trusted him—had even left him the show in my will."

"That's it!" exclaimed Clark. "It all ties up with the rest. Morgan is the murderer."

"But how could he be?" asked the carnival owner, gazing at the still figure of the white-haired man. "Morgan had black hair and a full face. Look how those cheeks are sunken, and his hair is white. Besides, Morgan had a ring that he couldn't get off—and we found that ring on the headless man."

"That was where the catch came in," said Clark. "I didn't know he couldn't get it off until he had filed it. You see, I found the filings."

"But the hair and the face?" protested Shreve. "How do you explain that?"

"This man wore a cleverly made black wig, and the reason his face looks so different now is that his double set of false teeth are missing," Clark smiled. "That makes a very drastic change in a man's appearance."

"See here," bellowed the captain of the State Troopers. "What's this all about?"

"That fellow on the floor is an escaped convict," stated Clark.

At that the knife-thrower groaned.

"I'll say he is," he murmured. "His name's Whitey Everetts."

"Good," said Clark. "This convict, Whitey Everetts, was Fred Morgan to everyone in the show. He got into your good graces, Shreve, because he worked faithfully and you thought he was loyal to you and the show. But he was really running a dope racket on the side through some of his good friends he wormed into the outfit. That worked out all right for a while, then he got delusions of grandeur."

"What do you mean by that?" demanded the carnival owner.

"I'll try and explain," continued Clark. "Somehow—probably through handling the correspondence—Everetts discovered there was a mortgage on this show. He bought that mortgage with his drug profits, but he wasn't out for just the interest. He could do that without you knowing it, Shreve, because the bank was insolvent and in the hands of the receivers.

"He had to make the show go broke so that you either couldn't meet your interest or you couldn't pay your bills. In the first case he'd foreclose. In the second case he'd buy out the auction with his mortgage.

"Then, one day, you found out that drugs were being peddled from the show, though you did not know who was doing it. You dictated a letter to Morgan, or Everetts, which was sent to Washington, requesting that a man from the Narcotics Squad join the carnival and investigate." Clark looked at Shreve. "Is that right?"

"By God, that is." Shreve gazed at him in amazement. "He knew who you were all the time."

"Sure," said Clark. "So he had to get rid of his dope business or he had to get rid of me. He tried to murder me several times. His failures made him desperate.

"Besides, he was getting to the end of the string. He was afraid that his men might talk—and he was afraid that his black wig might be discovered. The only thing he could do would be to have himself believed dead in the Morgan role. That would ease him out of the picture. But he couldn't substitute a body that didn't look like him, so he had to cut off the head. He'd brought back those headhunters, and he knew some of their language, so he hit on the idea of turning them loose.

"That would, he thought, divert suspicion from himself. He could commit the murders, hide the headhunters, and later turn them over or get them caught and hanged for the crimes. That way he was able to dispose of the two men who were in the dope business with him before they could talk to me."

"You mean the barkers at the headhunter show and the House of Horror?"

"Yes," the detective nodded. "The knife-thrower was to be

the third victim. He was about to be killed when I came in. He is part of the dope gang."

"Yeah?" growled the knife-thrower.

"Exactly," said Clark. He frowned as he glanced at the carnival owner. "How long ago did you make out that will leaving the show to Morgan?"

"Why, a few days ago," answered Shreve. "But I only told Morgan about it after we had learned of that first murder."

"And he probably intended you to be the fourth victim," stated Clark. "After you had been killed, Morgan would come back. He'd say we had made a mistake in thinking he had been that third headless corpse we found, and take over the show.

"But he slipped up. They all do. He hid the dope in the hollow knife handles, and I got one." Clark paused and looked down as he discovered the white-haired man's eyes were open and he was staring up vindictively. "I knew then who your third ally was, and I knew I'd find you with him. That body you changed clothes with was that of a working man. The hands were calloused. Furthermore, you always wore a big square ring on your index finger. Rings leave a mark on a man's hand. You couldn't get that ring off intact, so you had to saw it off. I found the filings."

"What sort of a ring was it?" asked the captain of the troopers.

"It was an odd looking Spanish affair," continued Clark. "With sharp edges to the stone. The ring left that mark on young McDonald's face here when he fought with Everetts."

"Who's this McDonald?"

"He has been after Everetts. He tried for him whenever he spotted him, hoping to get him. It so happened that I spotted Everetts at the same time and had to tangle with McDonald.

"McDonald thought I was after him, which I was not. He was ready to kill to keep from being burned, and I don't blame him, particularly as he wasn't guilty of the crime he's charged with. He's here to get the man who killed his father."

Clark glared at the white-haired man.

"Listen, Everetts—I've got the goods on you plenty. You'll sizzle. But that isn't any reason this kid should go along with you. Did you kill McDonald?"

"Sure," snarled Whitey Everetts, alias Morgan. "What of it? I did it."

"That settles it," smiled Clark. "Now, people, if you don't mind, this has been a pretty strenuous night for me. I think I rate some sleep."

Still smiling, he stepped out of the door and went along the deserted midway, where everything was now strangely peaceful. He knew what his report would say:

Peddling suppressed.
Robert W. Clark.

THE DEATH FLYER

The Death Flyer

L OST deep in the ebon tangle and echoing against the starless, sullen sky, the owl's dismal chatter came like the rattle in a dying man's throat.

Jim Bellamy paused on the ties, the beat of his heart surging through his throat. The hoot of an owl meant that someone would die.

He forced a smile to his lips at that and shrugged, setting off again through the lonesome tangle which matted the ancient and decayed tracks. He had been a fool to start back this late. He might fall into a hole or through a rotten trestle and break his neck.

But for all his smile, his big shoulders were hunched under his checkered flannel shirt and the scuff of his calks on the gritty cinders fell upon his ears like thunder in the silence.

He had not particularly enjoyed this job of surveying, but in these days, a civil engineer had to take what he could get, even though it meant the tangles and swamps and insects of northern Maine.

He had overstayed himself, checking over his shots. He had sent his crew back to their isolated lumber camp. If anything happened to him that he could not return, they would merely assume that he had chosen to spend the night in the open.

And an inner self or outer self kept telling him that

73

something would happen, that this night was not like other nights. A vibration of unrest was in the air.

He stumbled along the tracks he could not see, and blessed them and cursed them in one breath. This railroad had been deserted for about ten years. Why, he could not exactly remember. Something about their rolling stock going up in smoke. Some wreck or other, he supposed.

Now that his mind was started along that channel, he persisted in digging out fragmentary details of what he had heard. Loggers talk and a civil engineer pretends to listen. Loggers were a superstitious lot, given to tall imaginings.

Yes, he remembered what had happened now. A train had gone through a bridge into a swollen stream and the road had never been able to rebuild for lack of funds and interest on the part of shippers who remembered the incident. It was a shame for all this work to go to waste this way. Rails and ties were still there, all in place. No one in this forgotten forest had had any use for them.

The owl gave his death rattle again. Jim Bellamy quickened his pace. Suddenly he tripped. His stomach felt light. He heard a growing roar reverberate through the trees.

When he tried to get up he was blinded by a yellow eye which grew larger and larger with the noise. He rolled to one side but he could not get off the tracks.

Something was holding his shirt, pinning him down, and the yellow eye stabbed straight through him and held him horror-stricken to the ties.

Good God, it was a train and he was in its path!

He shut his eyes tightly. The roar shook the earth and

through it he seemed to hear the call of the owl which had foretold his death.

A shrill screech bit through the roar and then the thunder died to a hiss. Jim Bellamy sat up. Somehow he was no longer on the track but beside it. A mountain of rust-eaten steel reared up before him. Flame licked out and illuminated a cab. A shadowy face peered down.

"Y'all right, stranger?"

"Sure," said Bellamy in a shaky voice. "Sure. I'm all right."

"Well then, why the hell don't you get aboard? You think I've got all night?"

"Sure," said Bellamy, stumbling up to the tender.

"Not here, you fool. What do ya think we got coaches for? Get back there and get aboard. I'm in a hurry tonight. D'you realize it's a quarter past nine?"

Dazedly, Bellamy went back along the line of weather-beaten wooden coaches. Through the dirty windows he could see faces peering curiously at him. The lights which burned in the train, thought Bellamy with a start, threw no reflection on the ground.

He swung himself up into a vestibule which smelled of cinders and soft coal gas and stale cigars and opened the door into a coach. The old-fashioned lamps threw a dismal greenish light along the scarred red plush seats. Half a dozen silent passengers stared moodily ahead, paying him no heed.

Bellamy slid into a seat near the door. The engine panted, the couplings clanked as the engineer took up the slack and then the train went rolling off along the uneven bed.

Bellamy found that he could not think clearly or connectedly.

The fall must have given him a nasty crack on the head. Maybe it was worse than he had thought.

He sat motionless for some time. Of his fellow travelers he could see little more than the backs of their heads. There was something unnatural about the way they sat. Tense was the word. Tense and expectant.

A man with dull, corroded brass buttons slouched into the car. His cap was pulled far down over his face and in his gloved hands he held a battered ticket puncher. He came back to where Bellamy sat.

"Ticket, please," and the voice was weary.

Bellamy sat up straight, staring at the face over him. The flesh hung in loose gouts from under the eyes. The teeth were broken behind black lips. A scar on the forehead bled down over the gray flesh but no blood touched the floor. The eyes were unseen, merely black holes in the ashen putty.

Bellamy recovered his voice. "I have no ticket."

The empty voice whined a little. "You're a new one. I never saw you before. We're late now and I can't stop to put you off."

Bellamy fumbled with the breast pocket of his checkered flannel shirt. "I'll give you the money."

"Money? I have no need of money. Not now. All I want is your ticket. Haven't you got a ticket?"

Bellamy detected a motion farther up the car. He saw that the six passengers were getting slowly to their feet and coming back.

They ranged themselves behind the conductor, staring at Bellamy. The air was charged with an evil, decayed smell.

Bellamy came halfway to his feet, gripping the edges of the seat, his face blanching.

Not one of those six had visible eyes. Their flesh was the color of dirty lard. Their lips were black and their faces were slashed with many cuts.

A small man, older than the rest, better dressed, pointed a thin, clattering finger at Bellamy. "He is not one of us. He doesn't belong here!"

Bellamy moved closer to the window. The conductor stood to one side. The six, hands loose at their sides, moved slowly ahead, swaying and jolting under the influence of the train.

It was several seconds before Bellamy understood what they were trying to do. Then he realized that their unseen eyes held the threat of death.

He stood up, crouching forward, and though his face was white, his jaw was stubbornly set.

A lanky thing reached him first. Bellamy lashed out with his fist and rocked the tall body back into the others. But they came slowly on as though they hadn't seen. The lanky one was with them again.

Bellamy felt like a trapped animal about to be mangled by a hunter. Big as he was, he was no match for six. Fleshless hands reached out and gripped him. Bodies pressed him back.

He struck as hard as he could, twisting and writhing to get away.

Suddenly, above the clatter of steel wheels on rails, a clear, controlled voice said, "Let him be. He does not know."

The six fell away, backing into the aisle, looking neither to the right nor the left. They were like marionettes on strings, jiggling loosely as the train swayed.

Bellamy braced himself and rubbed at his throat where red marks were beginning to appear. Looking through the six, he was startled to see a young girl in a flame-colored dress poised in the aisle.

Her cheeks were as white as flour, but there was a certain beauty about her which Bellamy could not at once define. She was small, not over five feet four in height. The dress clung to her smooth body and rippled as she moved. Her eyes were dark and sad.

"Go back to your seats," she said.

The six moved woodenly to their places and seated themselves without a backward glance. But the conductor stood his ground.

"He has no ticket," said the conductor.

"I have it," replied the girl with a tired sigh. "I have had it for a long, long while."

She reached into a small red purse she carried and drew out a crumpled green slip which she handed to the man with the corroded brass buttons. He scanned it, and then punched it with a quick snap.

She watched him open the door and disappear and then she came slowly toward Bellamy and, reaching slowly out, took his hands in hers and sank down across from him, searching his face.

"You do not remember," she said gently.

Bellamy shook his head. He was too astonished to answer her immediately. Now that she was near to him he could smell the delicate odor of lilies of the valley. Her fine face was uptilted to him and her hands were shaking.

"I have waited long," she said. "For ten years. And now you have come. I knew that it would be you. The waiting was long but now that you are here, I see that the time was nothing. Please, don't you remember?"

He could make no answer to her even flow of words. He felt somehow that he should know, that he should remember, but his mind was dull.

"Remember how you wired me?" she went on. "How you said, 'Whenever you come, I shall be here on this platform, waiting for you'? And now I see that you have tired of waiting and that you have come to me. You see . . . I could not come to you. I must stay here with these. It is hard sometimes, harder than you know. But now all that is past and you are with me again."

She raised her slim hand to his face and touched his cheeks. "You are not changed . . . and though I cannot see you . . . very well, just to feel you is enough. Please never go away again. I have been so lonely, I have waited so long."

Bellamy felt as though someone had thrust a dagger into his heart and twisted it there. This girl was almost blind. He was afraid to answer her, afraid that his voice would dispel the illusion she cherished.

But speak he must and although the lump was large in his throat, he said, "No. I won't leave you . . . again."

Then somehow he had gathered her close to him and she was vibrant against him and her breath was warm and sweet upon his face. He held her there for a long time.

"Then it is you after all," she murmured. "I waited so long."

The conductor came back, staring at his nickel-plated watch. "He'll make it. He'll make it. But there's only half an hour left."

The girl shivered against Bellamy. "Must it happen again, now that—"

"Must what happen?" Bellamy demanded with a sudden clarity of mind. He felt like a hypnotized person returning to life.

"Why . . . why, the wreck, of course. But then you would not know about that. You were waiting. You were not with me then."

The conductor snapped shut the watch and moved heavily up the car, muttering, "He'll make it."

"The wreck?" said Bellamy.

"Yes. This is August the sixteenth, isn't it? Certainly it must be, otherwise we would not be out. August the sixteenth is the date, don't you see? Ten years ago tonight. I hate it but there is nothing I can do. Wait, dearest. Wait. Perhaps you can stop it. If anyone does, then it will be over."

Bellamy felt his mind grow leaden again. But he stood up, pressing her back into the seat. His eyes were staring and his jaw was set. He knew that somehow this was all wrong, that this couldn't be happening. But it was.

"In ten minutes, *they'll* come aboard. *They'll* hang out a red lantern and we'll stop. If you could make them . . ."

Bellamy stared down at her. His heart was pounding against his ribs and he labored with a problem he could not understand.

A red lantern, eh? And somehow everything would be all

right if he could stop this thing. He leaned quickly over her and kissed her soft, moist lips. Then he went up the car past the six passengers. They were still leaning forward staring with their sunken sockets and seeing nothing.

Bellamy swung open the door, walked across the swinging vestibule, pushed open another door and found himself in a baggage car.

The baggage man stared at him and nodded. The baggage man's face was a black shadow and his hands were white and thin.

"What's the use, mister?" said the baggage man. "You can't stop them."

Bellamy swung on by and went through a door. He crawled up over the tender and looked down on the cab. The fireman was throwing coal into the box, sweat standing out and shining in the light. The fireman worked like a machine and the flames belched redly from the open door.

The engineer turned to stare at Bellamy and Bellamy stared back. The engineer's face was nothing but a shadow on which was perched the billed cap of his kind. The engineer's hand was on the throttle, easing it back.

"You can't do anything," said the engineer. "Look out. I gotta stop."

The fireman shoveled with jerky regularity. Bellamy, standing with the firelight hot on his face, said, "Why don't you try? Just this once. Then—"

"It's no use, mister. I've tried it and I can't. That's a red lantern and a flag stop. I got my orders."

Bellamy saw the man haul on the brake. Steam hissed, steel

wheels groaned as they slid on the rails. Bellamy saw they were drawing up to a platform overgrown with long weeds. The station house had gradually collapsed into itself until only a few boards were left—a few boards and the drooping roof beam like a gallows against the sullen sky. An ancient sign creaked and banged in the wind. Once again Bellamy heard the call of the owl and shivered.

Suddenly, beside the cab there appeared a shock of black hair. The man reached for the rungs and swung up to the cab, followed by two other men more ragged and dirty than he.

The first one was tall and thick through the body like a carelessly filled bag of rags. His teeth were yellow and his eyes blazed.

"Pull out," said the man. "I'm riding here."

"You can't ride here," cried the engineer.

"Who's to say I can't?"

"I say you can't. Not unless you've got the orders tonight."

"What do I care for orders?" The thick one pulled a heavy, sawed-off shotgun from his coat and pointed it at the engineer.

The fireman jumped forward, shovel raised. The gun roared flame redder than the firebox. A black hole went through the fireman's guts. He fell heavily, clawing at the hot plates, sagging against the boilers. The rank, sickening odor of burning flesh filled the air. One hand was out of sight in the flames.

The engineer jammed the throttle ahead. The train lurched and started. The thick one was laughing and Bellamy smelled whiskey, cheap and strong, upon the fellow's breath. It had happened so fast that he could do nothing.

The gun roared flame redder than the firebox.
A black hole went through the fireman's guts.

The engineer was reaching for his hip pocket where a wrench bulged. One of the others yelled a warning. The thick one sent a roaring blast of flame and lead straight into the engineer's face. The man sank across his throttles, throwing them wider.

Bellamy was sick with the cold brutality of it. But the scatter-gun was empty and he saw no other weapons. He jerked up the fireman's shovel and aimed a blow at the thick one's skull.

The other two, their faces gray blots in the red flame, leaped ahead to snatch at the handle. Bellamy avoided them. The thick one fumbled for shells.

Bellamy yelled with rage and twisted the shovel free. He saw a blackjack come up with a swift, lethal swing. He dodged. The two men he faced laughed and weaved drunkenly. The blackjack landed at the base of Bellamy's neck.

Bellamy stumbled. A fist jarred into his chest. He doubled up, almost out, still trying to fight them back. The big one brought down the muzzle of the scatter-gun and kicked Bellamy back under the fireman's seat.

Then the three crawled up over the tender and stood for a moment against the sky, shouting at each other to be heard above the roar of the speeding train.

Bellamy, sick and dizzy, crawled out from the corner. He could not think of anything but the girl. These three drunken men were going back toward her. He had heard a snatch of their shouts. That had been enough.

His head was ringing and he could not concentrate. He

had the feeling that he was doing wrong to leave the cab but he could not reason why. The engineer was hanging against the throttles, but Bellamy did not understand.

Bellamy crawled up the tender and hitched himself over the coal and down toward the baggage car. He shoved open the door with shaking hands.

The baggage master was sprawled among the shifting trunks. His hands were outstretched and he did not move. The cashbox was standing open, keys jingling in the padlock.

Bellamy went on back. In the vestibule of the first coach he tripped over a sodden lump. He did not stop to inspect it. He plunged on through the empty coach to the second.

His brain was spinning like a maelstrom when he passed through the second vestibule and then his mind went clear again. He peered through the filthy pane of glass.

How long had he been at this? How much time had passed? Somehow that was important above all else.

The passengers were pressed back against the wall. With his scatter-gun in hand, the thick one held them at bay while his two companions went through pockets and grips. Their shouts were loud and harsh and their faces laughed but not their eyes.

Inside the coach, Bellamy saw a fire ax in its bracket on the wall. Cautiously, he moved the door inward. The thick one's back was toward him but at any moment one of the passengers might give a sign. One shot at that range from the scatter-gun . . .

And then Bellamy saw the girl. She was pressed far back

against the rearmost seat, her body tense, her hands thrown back in fear. The thick one reached out with a hard hand and jerked her toward him with a bellowed laugh.

He twisted her wrist until she knelt in the aisle and then, holding the scatter-gun loosely in one hand, he shifted his grip and snatched at her shoulder. Her lips went white with pain. The thick one laughed again.

"Hold her!" he shouted to his aides.

Bellamy was through the door, ax clutched in his two strong hands.

Suddenly the girl whipped free. The thick one's knuckles crashed against her eyes. She screamed and sank back on her knees, sinking down into the aisle.

A mad, mad thought raced through Bellamy's brain. So that's why she was blind.

He raced the length of the car. One of the aides shouted a warning. The thick one whirled, hair streaming down over his bloated gray face. His yellow teeth flashed and the heavy folds of ashy flesh jumped as he moved.

The scatter-gun was coming up. Bellamy lashed down with the ax. The blade bit cleanly through the matted hair, through the skull, deep into the face. But the big one stood and the wound did not bleed.

The aides screamed and ran, flashing out through the rear door, but the passengers stood with hands still upraised, without expression or movement.

The thick one tottered backward, clawing at the ax, knees buckling. He stumbled out through the door and out of sight.

Bellamy kneeled beside the girl, lifting her gently and holding her against him.

"It's all right," she whispered. "It's all right. You have come at last. I gave them your ticket here. Perhaps . . . perhaps . . . after this there will be . . . but the train! Good God, stop the train!"

Bellamy stared blankly at her without understanding. She clutched at his shirt, raising herself up. "Please, God, please don't let him go again. Please let him stop this. Please!"

She buried her face in his shirt and moaned. Suddenly a brain not Bellamy's took command of him. He started up and faced to the front. He saw the picture of the engineer slouched against the throttles.

Running, he went up the aisle, through the door and down the second coach. He could feel the wheels lifting from the curves under the onslaught of too much speed. The train swayed drunkenly from side to side, threatening to leave the tracks at any moment.

He was aware of someone behind him and he turned back. The girl in red was coming, groping blindly up the aisle, trying to keep up with him.

He swung her into his arms and stepped out into the vestibule. The dead conductor moved restlessly as the train swayed. In the baggage car the baggage master was pinned down under an upset trunk. His arms were still outstretched.

Bellamy pushed the girl up to the tender and followed her. The rocketing perch was hard to hold. Bellamy slid down into the cab. He heard the girl's scream.

Pulling the engineer away from the throttles, he clutched

them and hauled back. He tried to find the brake and could not. Some lever here was the brake. Something on this boiler or in this cab would stop the train. He tripped over the fireman's body and fell heavily, struggling up even before he hit.

The girl cried out again, her hands on his shoulders, trying to drag him to his feet.

"The trestle!" she cried.

He gripped her arms and looked into her drawn face. It was too late for brakes. Too late for anything.

The front trucks left the rails. The roar of water was under them, far under them. The train went off slowly, slowly, disjointed and lashing.

Space was greedy, sucking the cars down.

Holding the girl close to him, Bellamy braced himself against the crash. He could feel her quiver against him, he could hear the moan of agony which came from her tight throat.

The thunder and crushed steel, the roar of escaping steam, the splinter of rended wood, was suddenly swallowed by the cry of swirling water.

"Don't . . . don't go away from me!"

The voice receded, growing fainter and fainter until it was gone. In its place was the whisper of water against the sand.

Rough hands brought Bellamy to his feet. Daylight blinded him and he was aware of an ache which sent quick lightning flashes through his head when he moved.

Through the swirl of faces about him he could see a crumpled ruin against the bank from which protruded a rust-eaten set of trucks. Farther along he could see the hulk of an old locomotive, bent and twisted and brown under the clear sun.

His eyes focused on the faces and a single thought shot a question from him. "What . . . have they . . . where is she?"

"He's balmy," remarked a rodman Bellamy suddenly recognized as his own.

"You'd be balmy too, I guess," retorted a recorder in great heat.

Bellamy's camp cook was feeling Bellamy's head. "It's all right. He ain't hurt none to speak about."

"But the wreck!" pleaded Bellamy.

"What wreck?" said the recorder. "You mean this old train here. That fell off the trestle about ten years ago, I reckon. That's what made 'em shut this line down. About ten years ago it was, and, I think, about this time of the year. But you ain't been in no wreck, Bel. You stumbled off that trestle in the dark and lit in the soft sand. Some drop, ain't it? We been looking for you all morning, but you ain't hurt none."

"You went a hell of a ways past the lumber camp," said the cook. "What was the matter? Soused? Don't tell us you got lost."

"I . . . guess I did," said Bellamy, feeling very weak and dizzy and somehow very sad.

"C'mon," said the rodman, "we'll tote you back to camp. Hell, unless you get well right quick, we'll lose two days or more."

"We…won't lose anything," said Bellamy. "I guess we better be getting back to the job."

"Okay with us," said the recorder and helped Bellamy walk up the steep bank. "But I think you'd better lay up for a while. You must have been out for a long time and that ain't so good."

Bellamy stopped at the top and looked back at the old wreck half buried in the sand and water. It was rusty and broken and forgotten, somehow forlorn.

A voice seemed to whisper in his ear, "I will be waiting . . . on the other side. The next time we'll get through."

He looked about him, startled, but his survey crew was silent, waiting for him to go on.

He stepped off down the uneven trail and vanished in the twilight of the woods.

STORY PREVIEW

NOW that you've just ventured through some of the captivating tales in the Stories from the Golden Age collection by L. Ron Hubbard, turn the page and enjoy a preview of *Mouthpiece*. Join young Mat Lawrence, the engineer son of a murdered gangster. With the "help" of his father's fast-talking criminal attorney, Mat stalks the murderers and a million dollars gone missing—a sure recipe for bullets, lies and bedlam.

MOUTHPIECE

SWARTZ made a tent out of his fat fingers and then moved them up to tug at his lower lip, his eyes warily regarding Mat. "All right, I'll tell you. Rat-Face O'Connell was on his trail. Your father had the dyeing and cleaning protection racket of this town and Rat-Face and his boys didn't like it. So, one night they went up to your father's apartment, shot down the guards and took Lawrence for a ride. That's the story."

Mat probed into the man's face as though searching for flaws. "Rat-Face O'Connell, eh?" He looked musingly into the palm of his hand as if it were a textbook. "Rat-Face O'Connell. All right, where does he hang around?"

"Oh no, no!" cried Swartz.

"Oh yes, yes!" disputed Mat. "Where can I find him, now—tonight?"

"But . . . but," blubbered Swartz. "It's . . . it's suicide, Mr. Lawrence. I can't let you do it." He whipped out a polka dot handkerchief and mopped at his brow as though the idea had turned the room into a furnace. "You'd better get out and leave this thing alone!"

"I suppose I'm a yellowbelly. Like the rest of you guys, eh?" Mat threw a twisted smile at Swartz. "Well, you're wrong.

If you think anybody can bump my dad and then get off scot-free, you're cockeyed as hell."

His square jaw jutted out and his eyes were the size of match heads. "I'm looking to get Mr. Rat-Face and make him talk. Talk, get me? He'll burn for that night's work, or by God, I'll take him to hell with me."

"Wheeoo!" breathed Swartz, mopping ever harder. He fanned himself with the silk, leaning back in the chair. It was as though he had cooled his legal brain, for he suddenly crouched forward, confidential and wise. "How much money have you got, Mr. Lawrence?"

"Oh, I see!" snapped Mat. "I've got to pay for the dope."

"No," purred Swartz, "you haven't. I'm going to give you the address. The dough is for a couple of your father's gorillas to go with you. You remember them. Petey and Blake."

Mat sought for the answer in his palm and after several moments of concentrated searching, looked up. "All right. I've got five hundred bucks. That will cover Petey, Blake and a car. You're going to lend me a gat."

"Fine." Swartz leaned back again. "I'll send them around at seven to your hotel. Where are you stopping?"

"Oh, I guess the Savoy is as good as any. Now," he got up to leave, "where are my dad's papers? I want to read them over and find out what the score was."

Swartz gave Mat a sad stare. "The papers were all taken by O'Connell and his boys. He didn't leave anything with me, ever."

Mat frowned and then walked to the door, placing his

huge hand on the knob. "I'll be back and see you tomorrow, Swartz, if I live to tell the yarn."

Sharply at seven a black sedan stood courteously at the entrance of the Savoy Hotel, two men in the front seat. Mat Lawrence loomed out of the lighted doorway, towering over the gilt-frogged doorman, and looked into the car. He saw Petey first. "Hello, Petey. Hello, Blake."

Petey was mostly chest and his head resembled nothing so much as a shoe box sunk into his torso—green buttons for eyes and a ragged knife gash for a mouth. Blake was oily and sleek, his hair glistening more than his patent leather shoes, and his black eyes shinier than either. They gave Mat a heartless "Hello" and glanced at each other.

"Get in back, mugs," commanded Mat. "I'm driving."

Grudgingly, shying away from the bright lights of the entrance as though they stung, Petey and Blake squirmed out and slunk into the back seat.

Three sizes too big for the seat, Mat crumped the gears and stabbed the headlights out into the blur of traffic. "Where do we go?"

Petey leaned forward, his voice rasping like a saw in mahogany. "Head straight out this street, bo. I'll put ya wise to the turns." He glanced at Blake before he sat back and Blake nodded, his lips sliding into a knowing smile as though well oiled.

With a turn here and a curve there, the sedan went on through the glaring city until the house windows were more dimly lighted and the houses themselves seemed to exude darkness. Mat found it hard to distinguish streets from alleys.

"Hey, Petey," he called over his shoulder. "Where's the gun Swartz sent?"

Petey slid an automatic pistol across the rear seat. Mat looked at the blue glint and then shoved the weapon into his coat, to slip out the clip and find that it was fully loaded.

"Thanks, Petey." He glanced up into the rearview mirror. "Say, what the hell are you smiling about?"

"Oh, things," rasped Petey. "You turn down this next one."

Suddenly uncomfortable as if he were hearing fingernails scraping over a blackboard, Mat turned the designated corner and found that he was leaving the last of the houses behind him.

He humped over the wheel, speeding up.

"Say, Petey," he hurled over his shoulder. "Were you in at Dad's finish?"

Leaning forward, Petey obliged. "Nope, I arrived about ten minutes afterwards. This Rat-Face O'Connell had cleared out with most of the papers and all the loose jack. I been itchin' ta get my mitts on him ever since."

He pointed with a dirty finger. "Ya turn down that next road there. The little one."

"Okay." Mat did as he was directed. "This bird sure lives a helluva ways out, doesn't he? Listen, I'm going to drive right up in front of the house. You two birds circle around back and try to get in that way. After that we'll see what we'll see. Get me?"

"Sure," said Petey.

96

"If I'm right, this Rat-Face is a rotten shot. And I want him alive, get that? Alive! He's going to burn, see?"

"Sure," said Petey.

"Say!" Mat sat up suddenly and slowed down. "This is the city dump!"

"Sure!" said Petey. "Slow down and stop." He pressed a gat into Mat's ear where it bored viciously. "You didn't know it, bo, but you was takin' yerself fer a ride!"

To find out more about *Mouthpiece* and how you can obtain your copy, go to www.goldenagestories.com.

GLOSSARY

STORIES FROM THE GOLDEN AGE *reflect the words and expressions used in the 1930s and 1940s, adding unique flavor and authenticity to the tales. While a character's speech may often reflect regional origins, they also can convey attitudes common in the day. So that readers can better grasp such cultural and historical terms, uncommon words or expressions of the era, the following glossary has been provided.*

---

ballyhoo: one who clamorously and vigorously attempts to win customers; to make publicity.

barker: someone who stands in front of a show at a carnival and gives a loud colorful sales talk to potential customers.

blackjack: a short, leather-covered club, consisting of a heavy head on a flexible handle, used as a weapon.

bo: pal; buster; fellow.

bulls: cops; police officers.

bump: kill.

calks: the spiked plates fixed on the bottoms of shoes to prevent slipping and to preserve the soles.

cribbage: a card game for from two to four players in which the score is kept by inserting small pegs into holes arranged in rows on a small board.

dick: a detective.

dint of, by: by means of.

finis: the end; the conclusion.

Flyer: a passenger express train.

foppish: of a fop, a man who is excessively concerned with his clothes and appearance.

gat: gun.

gilt-frogged: a garment having gold ornamental fastenings that consists of a button and the loop through which it passes.

G-men: Government men; agents of the Federal Bureau of Investigation.

grifter: crooked game operator; a person who operates a sideshow at a circus, fair, etc., especially a gambling attraction.

grinder: grind man; usually the ticket seller, who would give a rhythmic and continuous spiel meant to move patrons into the show.

haymakers: powerful blows with the fists.

honky-tonk: a style of ragtime music with a heavy beat, usually played on an upright piano with a tinny sound.

husky: a big, strong person.

jack: money.

lam, take it on the: the act or an instance of escaping, as from confinement or difficulty.

midway: an avenue or area at a carnival along which or in which are concessions for exhibitions of curiosities, games of chance, scenes from foreign life, merry-go-rounds and other rides and amusements.

mitts: hands.

motley: consisting of people that are very different from one another and do not seem to belong together.

mouthpiece: a criminal lawyer.

mugs: hoodlums; thugs; criminals.

nailers: the police in general; police officers.

pasteboards: tickets for admission; visiting cards.

phrenologist's chart: an illustration of the human head, divided into a grid on which each section represents different personality traits. It was used in the practice of phrenology which is a theory that claims to be able to determine character, personality traits and criminality on the basis of the shape of the head. The overlying skull bone was believed to reflect the different mental faculties of the mind, each of which were represented in a different part of the brain.

property men: propmen; men who look after stage properties.

put ya wise: tell you; give you the information.

receivers: someone, or several people, appointed by a court to manage a business or property that is involved in a legal process such as bankruptcy.

recorder: a survey party's noteman; the member of a survey team whose job it is to assist surveyors in measuring angles, distances and elevations, and to record the measurements.

rodman: in surveying, a person who carries the leveling rod, a light pole marked with gradations, held upright and read through a surveying instrument.

rolling stock: locomotives, carriages or other vehicles used on a railway.

rube: a person from a rural area; a scornful term used to describe an outsider to show business; also *towner, townie, sucker* or *chump.*

scatter-gun: a shotgun; a firearm that is a double-barreled smoothbore shoulder weapon for firing shot at short ranges.

Scheherazade: the female narrator of *The Arabian Nights,* who during one thousand and one adventurous nights saved her life by entertaining her husband, the king, with stories.

shot his cuffs: shoot a cuff; lightly tug on the coat sleeve, causing the white cuff of the shirt to pop out slightly.

shots: estimations of distance or altitude by the use of a surveying instrument.

spieler: outside talker; the talker who convinces onlookers that they absolutely must see this show.

stateroom: a private room or compartment on a train, ship, etc.

Streets of Cairo, The: song created by Sol Bloom, a show business promoter who was the entertainment director of the Chicago World's Columbian Exposition of 1893, which celebrated the 400th anniversary of Christopher Columbus' discovery of the New World. One of its attractions, called Streets of Cairo, included the famous dancer Little Egypt, snake charmers, camel riders and other entertainment.

tender: a car attached to a locomotive and carrying a supply of fuel and water.

ties: any of a number of closely spaced beams of wood for holding the rails forming a train track at the proper distance from each other.

trainman: a member of the operating crew on a train, the method of conveyance for the carnival.

transom: a seat or couch built at the side of a cabin, usually with lockers or drawers underneath.

Treasury Department: an executive department of the US federal government that carries out certain law enforcement activities as one of its basic functions. One of its departments, the Financial Crimes Enforcement Network, helps law enforcement agencies and financial institutions to prevent and detect money laundering.

trestle: a kind of framework of strong posts or piles for supporting a bridge or the track of a railway.

trucks: train wheel unit; a swiveling frame that the wheels and springs are mounted on at either end of a railroad car.

L. Ron Hubbard
in the Golden Age
of Pulp Fiction

*In writing an adventure story
a writer has to know that he is adventuring
for a lot of people who cannot.
The writer has to take them here and there
about the globe and show them
excitement and love and realism.
As long as that writer is living the part of an
adventurer when he is hammering
the keys, he is succeeding with his story.*

*Adventuring is a state of mind.
If you adventure through life, you have a
good chance to be a success on paper.*

*Adventure doesn't mean globe-trotting,
exactly, and it doesn't mean great deeds.
Adventuring is like art.
You have to live it to make it real.*

— L. RON HUBBARD

L. Ron Hubbard
and American
Pulp Fiction

B ORN March 13, 1911, L. Ron Hubbard lived a life at least as expansive as the stories with which he enthralled a hundred million readers through a fifty-year career.

Originally hailing from Tilden, Nebraska, he spent his formative years in a classically rugged Montana, replete with the cowpunchers, lawmen and desperadoes who would later people his Wild West adventures. And lest anyone imagine those adventures were drawn from vicarious experience, he was not only breaking broncs at a tender age, he was also among the few whites ever admitted into Blackfoot society as a bona fide blood brother. While if only to round out an otherwise rough and tumble youth, his mother was that rarity of her time—a thoroughly educated woman—who introduced her son to the classics of occidental literature even before his seventh birthday.

But as any dedicated L. Ron Hubbard reader will attest, his world extended far beyond Montana. In point of fact, and as the son of a United States naval officer, by the age of eighteen he had traveled over a quarter of a million miles. Included therein were three Pacific crossings to a then still mysterious Asia, where he ran with the likes of Her British Majesty's agent-in-place

L. Ron Hubbard, left, at Congressional Airport, Washington, DC, 1931, with members of George Washington University flying club.

for North China, and the last in the line of Royal Magicians from the court of Kublai Khan. For the record, L. Ron Hubbard was also among the first Westerners to gain admittance to forbidden Tibetan monasteries below Manchuria, and his photographs of China's Great Wall long graced American geography texts.

Upon his return to the United States and a hasty completion of his interrupted high school education, the young Ron Hubbard entered George Washington University. There, as fans of his aerial adventures may have heard, he earned his wings as a pioneering barnstormer at the dawn of American aviation. He also earned a place in free-flight record books for the longest sustained flight above Chicago. Moreover, as a roving reporter for *Sportsman Pilot* (featuring his first professionally penned articles), he further helped inspire a generation of pilots who would take America to world airpower.

Immediately beyond his sophomore year, Ron embarked on the first of his famed ethnological expeditions, initially to then untrammeled Caribbean shores (descriptions of which would later fill a whole series of West Indies mystery-thrillers). That the Puerto Rican interior would also figure into the future of Ron Hubbard stories was likewise no accident. For in addition to cultural studies of the island, a 1932–33

LRH expedition is rightly remembered as conducting the first complete mineralogical survey of a Puerto Rico under United States jurisdiction.

There was many another adventure along this vein: As a lifetime member of the famed Explorers Club, L. Ron Hubbard charted North Pacific waters with the first ship-board radio direction finder, and so pioneered a long-range navigation system universally employed until the late twentieth century. While not to put too fine an edge on it, he also held a rare Master Mariner's license to pilot any vessel, of any tonnage in any ocean.

Yet lest we stray too far afield, there is an LRH note at this juncture in his saga, and it reads in part:

"I started out writing for the pulps, writing the best I knew, writing for every mag on the stands, slanting as well as I could."

To which one might add: His earliest submissions date from the summer of 1934, and included tales drawn from true-to-life Asian adventures, with characters roughly modeled on British/American intelligence operatives he had known in Shanghai. His early Westerns were similarly peppered with details drawn from personal experience. Although therein lay a first hard lesson from the often cruel world of the pulps. His first Westerns were soundly rejected as lacking the authenticity of a Max Brand yarn

Capt. L. Ron Hubbard in Ketchikan, Alaska, 1940, on his Alaskan Radio Experimental Expedition, the first of three voyages conducted under the Explorers Club flag.

(a particularly frustrating comment given L. Ron Hubbard's Westerns came straight from his Montana homeland, while Max Brand was a mediocre New York poet named Frederick Schiller Faust, who turned out implausible six-shooter tales from the terrace of an Italian villa).

Nevertheless, and needless to say, L. Ron Hubbard persevered and soon earned a reputation as among the most publishable names in pulp fiction, with a ninety percent placement rate of first draft manuscripts. He was also among the most prolific, averaging between seventy and a hundred thousand words a month. Hence the rumors that L. Ron Hubbard had redesigned a typewriter for faster keyboard action and pounded out manuscripts on a continuous roll of butcher paper to save the precious seconds it took to insert a single sheet of paper into manual typewriters of the day.

That all L. Ron Hubbard stories did not run beneath said byline is yet another aspect of pulp fiction lore. That is, as publishers periodically rejected manuscripts from top-drawer authors if only to avoid paying top dollar, L. Ron Hubbard and company just as frequently replied with submissions under various pseudonyms. In Ron's case, the

A MAN OF MANY NAMES

Between 1934 and 1950, L. Ron Hubbard authored more than fifteen million words of fiction in more than two hundred classic publications. To supply his fans and editors with stories across an array of genres and pulp titles, he adopted fifteen pseudonyms in addition to his already renowned L. Ron Hubbard byline.

Winchester Remington Colt
Lt. Jonathan Daly
Capt. Charles Gordon
Capt. L. Ron Hubbard
Bernard Hubbel
Michael Keith
Rene Lafayette
Legionnaire 148
Legionnaire 14830
Ken Martin
Scott Morgan
Lt. Scott Morgan
Kurt von Rachen
Barry Randolph
Capt. Humbert Reynolds

list included: Rene Lafayette, Captain Charles Gordon, Lt. Scott Morgan and the notorious Kurt von Rachen—supposedly on the lam for a murder rap, while hammering out two-fisted prose in Argentina. The point: While L. Ron Hubbard as Ken Martin spun stories of Southeast Asian intrigue, LRH as Barry Randolph authored tales of

L. Ron Hubbard, circa 1930, at the outset of a literary career that would finally span half a century.

romance on the Western range—which, stretching between a dozen genres is how he came to stand among the 200 elite authors providing close to a million tales through the glory days of American Pulp Fiction.

In evidence of exactly that, by 1936 L. Ron Hubbard was literally leading pulp fiction's elite as president of New York's American Fiction Guild. Members included a veritable pulp hall of fame: Lester "Doc Savage" Dent, Walter "The Shadow" Gibson, and the legendary Dashiell Hammett—to cite but a few.

Also in evidence of just where L. Ron Hubbard stood within his first two years on the American pulp circuit: By the spring of 1937, he was ensconced in Hollywood, adopting a Caribbean thriller for Columbia Pictures, remembered today as *The Secret of Treasure Island.* Comprising fifteen thirty-minute episodes, the L. Ron Hubbard screenplay led to the most profitable matinée serial in Hollywood history. In accord with Hollywood culture, he was thereafter continually called upon

The 1937 Secret of Treasure Island, *a fifteen-episode serial adapted for the screen by L. Ron Hubbard from his novel,* Murder at Pirate Castle.

to rewrite/doctor scripts—most famously for long-time friend and fellow adventurer Clark Gable.

In the interim—and herein lies another distinctive chapter of the L. Ron Hubbard story—he continually worked to open Pulp Kingdom gates to up-and-coming authors. Or, for that matter, anyone who wished to write. It was a fairly unconventional stance, as markets were already thin and competition razor sharp. But the fact remains, it was an L. Ron Hubbard hallmark that he vehemently lobbied on behalf of young authors—regularly supplying instructional articles to trade journals, guest-lecturing to short story classes at George Washington University and Harvard, and even founding his own creative writing competition. It was established in 1940, dubbed the Golden Pen, and guaranteed winners both New York representation and publication in Jack Byrne's *Argosy*.

But it was John W. Campbell Jr.'s *Astounding Science Fiction* that finally proved the most memorable LRH vehicle. While every fan of L. Ron Hubbard's galactic epics undoubtedly knows the story, it nonetheless bears repeating: By late 1938, the pulp publishing magnate of Street & Smith was determined to revamp *Astounding Science Fiction* for broader readership. In particular, senior editorial director F. Orlin Tremaine called for stories with a stronger *human element*. When acting editor John W. Campbell balked, preferring his spaceship-driven

112

tales, Tremaine enlisted Hubbard. Hubbard, in turn, replied with the genre's first truly *character-driven* works, wherein heroes are pitted not against bug-eyed monsters but the mystery and majesty of deep space itself—and thus was launched the Golden Age of Science Fiction.

The names alone are enough to quicken the pulse of any science fiction aficionado, including LRH friend and protégé, Robert Heinlein, Isaac Asimov, A. E. van Vogt and Ray Bradbury. Moreover, when coupled with LRH stories of fantasy, we further come to what's rightly been described as the foundation of every modern tale of horror: L. Ron Hubbard's immortal *Fear.* It was rightly proclaimed by Stephen King as one of the very few works to genuinely warrant that overworked term "classic"—as in: *"This is a classic tale of creeping, surreal menace and horror. . . . This is one of the really, really good ones."*

L. Ron Hubbard 1948, among fellow science fiction luminaries at the World Science Fiction Convention in Toronto.

To accommodate the greater body of L. Ron Hubbard fantasies, Street & Smith inaugurated *Unknown*—a classic pulp if there ever was one, and wherein readers were soon thrilling to the likes of *Typewriter in the Sky* and *Slaves of Sleep* of which Frederik Pohl would declare: *"There are bits and pieces from Ron's work that became part of the language in ways very few other writers managed."*

And, indeed, at J. W. Campbell Jr.'s insistence, Ron was regularly drawing on themes from the Arabian Nights and

113

so introducing readers to a world of genies, jinn, Aladdin and Sinbad—all of which, of course, continue to float through cultural mythology to this day.

At least as influential in terms of post-apocalypse stories was L. Ron Hubbard's 1940 *Final Blackout*. Generally acclaimed as the finest anti-war novel of the decade and among the ten best works of the genre ever authored—here, too, was a tale that would live on in ways few other writers imagined.

Hence, the later Robert Heinlein verdict: "Final Blackout *is as perfect a piece of science fiction as has ever been written.*"

Like many another who both lived and wrote American pulp adventure, the war proved a tragic end to Ron's sojourn in the pulps. He served with distinction in four theaters and was highly decorated

Portland, Oregon, 1943; L. Ron Hubbard, captain of the US Navy subchaser PC 815.

for commanding corvettes in the North Pacific. He was also grievously wounded in combat, lost many a close friend and colleague and thus resolved to say farewell to pulp fiction and devote himself to what it had supported these many years—namely, his serious research.

But in no way was the LRH literary saga at an end, for as he wrote some thirty years later, in 1980:

"Recently there came a period when I had little to do. This was novel in a life so crammed with busy years, and I decided to amuse myself by writing a novel that was pure *science fiction."*

That work was *Battlefield Earth: A Saga of the Year 3000.* It was an immediate *New York Times* bestseller and, in fact, the first international science fiction blockbuster in decades. It was not, however, L. Ron Hubbard's magnum opus, as that distinction is generally reserved for his next and final work: The 1.2 million word *Mission Earth.*

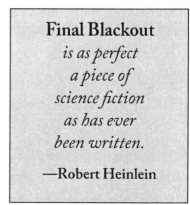

Final Blackout
*is as perfect
a piece of
science fiction
as has ever
been written.*

—Robert Heinlein

How he managed those 1.2 million words in just over twelve months is yet another piece of the L. Ron Hubbard legend. But the fact remains, he did indeed author a ten-volume *dekalogy* that lives in publishing history for the fact that each and every volume of the series was also a *New York Times* bestseller.

Moreover, as subsequent generations discovered L. Ron Hubbard through republished works and novelizations of his screenplays, the mere fact of his name on a cover signaled an international bestseller. . . . Until, to date, sales of his works exceed hundreds of millions, and he otherwise remains among the most enduring and widely read authors in literary history. Although as a final word on the tales of L. Ron Hubbard, perhaps it's enough to simply reiterate what editors told readers in the glory days of American Pulp Fiction:

He writes the way he does, brothers, because he's been there, seen it and done it!

THE STORIES FROM THE GOLDEN AGE

Your ticket to adventure starts here with the Stories from
the Golden Age collection by master storyteller L. Ron Hubbard.
These gripping tales are set in a kaleidoscope of exotic locales and brim
with fascinating characters, including some of the
most vile villains, dangerous dames and brazen heroes
you'll ever get to meet.

The entire collection of over one hundred and fifty stories is being
released in a series of eighty books and audiobooks.
For an up-to-date listing of available titles,
go to www.goldenagestories.com.

AIR ADVENTURE

Arctic Wings
The Battling Pilot
Boomerang Bomber
The Crate Killer
The Dive Bomber
Forbidden Gold
Hurtling Wings
The Lieutenant Takes the Sky

Man-Killers of the Air
On Blazing Wings
Red Death Over China
Sabotage in the Sky
Sky Birds Dare!
The Sky-Crasher
Trouble on His Wings
Wings Over Ethiopia

117

FAR-FLUNG ADVENTURE

SEA ADVENTURE

TALES FROM THE ORIENT

MYSTERY

FANTASY

SCIENCE FICTION

WESTERN

121

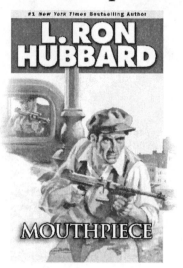

JOIN THE PULP REVIVAL
America in the 1930s and 40s

Pulp fiction was in its heyday and 30 million readers were regularly riveted by the larger than life tales of master storyteller L. Ron Hubbard. For this was pulp fiction's golden age, when the writing was raw and every page packed a walloping punch.

That magic can now be yours. An evocative world of nefarious villains, exotic intrigues, courageous heroes and heroines—a world that today's cinema has barely tapped for tales of adventure and swashbucklers.

Enroll today in the Stories from the Golden Age Club and begin receiving your monthly feature edition selected from more than 150 stories in the collection.

You may choose to enjoy them as either a paperback or audiobook for the special membership price of $9.95 each month along with FREE shipping and handling.

CALL TOLL-FREE: **1-877-8GALAXY**
(1-877-842-5299) OR GO ONLINE TO
www.goldenagestories.com
AND BECOME PART OF THE PULP REVIVAL!

Prices are set in US dollars only. For non-US residents, please call
1-323-466-7815 for pricing information. *Free shipping available for US residents only.

Galaxy Press, 7051 Hollywood Blvd., Suite 200, Hollywood, CA 90028